Lilli's
Quest

Lilli's Quest

Lila Perl

LIZZIE
SKURNICK
BOOKS

New York, New York

Printed in the United States of America.
10 9 8 7 6 5 4 3 2 1

No part of this book may be used or reproduced in any manner without written permission of the publisher. Please direct inquires to:

Lizzie Skurnick Books
an imprint of Ig Publishing
Box 2547
New York, NY 10163
www.igpub.com

ISBN: 978-163246-023-3 (hardcover)
ISBN: 978-1939601-53-7 (paperback)

PART I

1938-1942

One

Lilli wakes up to the sickly yellowish light of a November morning. They are still living in that high-ceilinged, ground-floor flat on Heinrichstrasse. The sun never pierces the tall, narrow windows and to Lilli, who hates the darkness, all of the rooms feel like the insides of brown-paper bags. It is 1938 and Lilli is eleven years old.

She and her younger sister Helga, who is ten, share a bed, very high and with tall, knobby bedposts that are carved with elaborate scrolls. The bed once belonged to Oma and Opa, their grandparents. Lilli's youngest sister Elspeth, now five, is still sleeping in her old baby cot, which is positioned crosswise at the foot of the family heirloom.

Today begins like an ordinary day. The girls of the Frankfurter family wake up, shiver as they wash themselves at the kitchen sink, and dress in their itchy woolen jumpers, thick black stockings, and sturdy oxfords.

They help Mutti prepare the family breakfast of hot milk, bread, and very small rations of jam, which is running short, as are many so-called luxury goods in

Germany in 1938. The country, under its Nazi dictator, Adolf Hitler, is arming not only for war in Europe but to take over the entire world. And Hitler's armies need to be equipped with the best of everything.

But war shortages aren't something that Lilli is thinking about right now. She's more concerned with thoroughly removing the despised skin that has formed on her mug of boiled milk. Mutti gazes at her frowning. "Always the same," she mutters in a tired voice. "You are throwing away nourishment, my child. It's hard enough to get milk these days, hard enough to keep body and soul together."

Lilli can't help noticing that Mutti, who was once so pretty, with her flaxen hair and flirtatious smile, has become faded, and that there is a faint new crease in her forehead. Papa, who has also come to the breakfast table, is dressed in his usual going-to-the-office suit. But in truth he won't be going anywhere. Many months ago, Papa was dismissed from his job as a chief scientist at a chemical plant near the town where the Frankfurters live.

When Papa arrived home in the middle of a workday, the astonished girls asked why. "You should already know the answer," Papa told them, not unkindly. "Why have all of you been forbidden to attend school with German children? Why did the Jewish school then burn down?"

Lilli flashed a bitter smile. "Of course, I know. They hate us, the Jews. What will you do now, Papa?"

There was no answer. Every day Papa dressed for the office. Sometimes he left the apartment and tried to find a job among his Jewish friends. Money had been saved but it was running low, and the Frankfurters had to borrow small sums from Mutti's family, the Bayers, who were not Jewish.

Papa responds to Mutti's criticism of Lilli. "Let the child indulge herself, Martina. Who knows what's coming?"

Papa is so handsome, in Lilli's opinion— his high cheekbones, the curl of his lips, his dark hair and amber-brown eyes, the richness in his deep voice.

Mutti has caught something in Papa's words. "You mean . . . ? Do you think there will be trouble today, Josef?"

Lilli's eyes and those of her sister Helga flash to the six-pointed yellow star with the word *Jude*, for Jew, which is sewn onto the sleeve of Papa's suit. If he goes into the streets searching for work, everyone will know that he belongs to the race that Hitler has sworn to wipe out. Already Jews in Germany have been stripped of their rights as citizens. They've been mocked, attacked, beaten, and even arrested. From her parents' conversation, Lilli senses that something truly evil may be coming.

Yet, the day goes by quietly enough. The older girls do their lessons with Papa instructing. Elspeth practices her alphabet and her reading, urged on by Mutti, and then goes off to play with her dolls. Papa reads the evening newspaper, which has been delivered to him by a kindly neighbor, Mr. Doppler, who is a so-called "pure" German and need not fear being questioned or even arrested by one of Hitler's special police.

Darkness descends and the girls go off to bed.

It is midnight, or perhaps later, when Lilli awakens to the sound of a distant roar that is punctuated with crashing sounds like those of china or glass being smashed and by the thudding noises of heavy objects being tossed from high places. She lies there for an unknowable time trying to make sense of what is happening. This isn't the first time that the Nazis have attacked Jewish-owned shops, homes, and schools. But this nighttime assault is much more terrifying than the usual daytime incidents.

Lilli nudges Helga, who sleeps on her stomach, her head sandwiched between two enormous goosedown pillows. "What, what?" Helga moans in annoyance.

"Oh, you are so deaf," Lilli scolds. "Get up and come with me to the window. Something terrible is happening. They are destroying everything that is Jewish. And the sounds are coming closer."

Barefoot, the girls tiptoe to the window so as not to wake Elspeth. Cautiously they lift a slat of the partially open wooden blinds for a fuller view. But all is darkness. "It's nothing," says Helga. "You and your dreams."

Lilli is furious enough to want to slap Helga, who is always so stolid and dull, has no imagination, and is never any fun. "Where are you going?" Lilli demands, as Helga prepares to go back to bed. "There is fire. I just saw it. Flames are lighting the sky and that awful noise is coming closer."

Helga doesn't answer and Lilli reluctantly follows her sister back to bed. She has no idea how long she's been lying there, eyes wide open in the dark, when she hears three sharp raps at the door of the apartment

Even Helga springs up and, in their long flannel nightgowns, the two girls race down the dark hallway to the parlor. To their surprise, the room is lit up, and Mutti and Papa are fully dressed, just as if they've been waiting for callers to arrive.

The "callers"—two of Hitler's secret-police agents—have already entered the Frankfurters' parlor. They both wear red armbands boldly advertising the well-known black swastika on a white background—the symbol of the Nazi Party. And they are armed with pistols.

Mutti rushes over to her daughters in an attempt to get them out of the room as quickly as possible. But Papa is right behind her. "No, let them stay!" He wrestles the girls free of Mutti and sits them down on the small brocade sofa against the wall. Helga has begun to sob quietly. Lilli holds her sister's hand tightly. The entire episode passes swiftly and as in a nightmare. The older officer, who

11

introduces himself as Captain Gerhardt Koeppler, tells Papa that he is under arrest and must come with them. When Mutti asks what Papa has done, no reason is given.

"Bring your papers," Koeppler barks at Papa "and if you have, a warm coat."

Mutti gives the pale-skinned Koeppler a pleading glance. "Surely, you need not take him away. He is the father of these children, and one more, the youngest who is only five . . ."

"I have my orders," the captain replies a bit less harshly. "You can come and ask for him at Gestapo headquarters. They will inform you."

Meekly, Mutti goes to get Papa's coat, and also gloves and a woolen muffler and hat. Papa comes to where Lilli and Helga are sitting and he kneels at their feet. His expression is fierce as he tells them, "Don't worry, my little loved ones. And above all, don't forget the reason for this terrible injustice. You must fight such hatred all your lives . . ."

Captain Koeppler has approached. He taps Papa on the shoulder, as he and the girls clasp one another in a teary embrace. Lilli knows one thing. She will never forget Papa's arm gripping her shoulder; she will never forget his lips on her wet cheek.

Lilli wakes up to lemony sunshine slanting through the attic window of the tall house in which she and

Mutti and her two sisters have been living for nearly six months, following that savage November night on Heinrichstrasse. The event has now come to be called *Kristallnacht*, or, in English, "Night of Broken Glass."

The destruction of Jewish property and the brutal arrests of Jewish men continued for a second night. Finally, on the third day, Mutti made her way to the secret-police quarters of the Gestapo. She walked through streets filled with the rubble of shattered windows, broken bricks and concrete, and smashed furniture. Even pianos had been thrown from the balconies of Jewish homes and apartments.

That day, and for many days afterward, Mutti was unable to learn anything of Papa's fate. The throng of mothers, wives, and daughters seeking information about their loved ones was so great that the building had been cordoned off. Oddly enough, it was a visit by Captain Koeppler to Heinrichstrasse that explained about Papa, and also gave Mutti and the girls "some good advice." Even on this sunny May morning, as Lilli gazes down onto the street from the turret-like chamber that she and Helga now occupy, she gets a wintry chill thinking of the Nazi officer's visit a few weeks after *Kristallnacht*.

Lilli and Helga were at their lessons at the big round table in the parlor under the supervision of Mutti when the doorbell rang. Mutti rose to answer it with both fear and hope. There could be a squadron of booted police come to search the apartment. On the other hand, there could be a helpful messenger with news of Papa.

Lilli looked up from her algebra studies to see a single uniformed figure emerging from the dim vestibule. Without Mutti saying a word, she and Helga leaped up and left the room. "It was *he*," Lilli whispered, as they hastened through the hallway to their bedroom, which they no longer shared with Elspeth. As the youngest member of the endangered family, she had already been taken to live with Oma Bayer in the big house in the aristocratic part of town.

"How could you be so sure?" Helga challenged. "You could not even see his face."

"I know him already," Lilli answered mysteriously. And soon after Mutti's caller had left, she came and confided to the girls that it had indeed been Captain Koeppler.

"How could you even talk to him?" Lilli demanded, "after he came here so . . . so roughly, and took Papa away?" It was then that Mutti gave them the news, trying to sound hopeful about Papa and even grateful to the tall, unsmiling Nazi officer.

At last they knew that after Papa had been taken into custody, he had been sent to a camp for political prisoners, where he would stay until his case had been reviewed. What was Papa's "case?" He had been accused of belonging to a group of Jews and other disloyal Germans trying to take back their rights as citizens and plotting against the Hitler government.

Helga began to sniff, but Lilli looked proud. "I knew Papa was no coward. He has nothing to be ashamed of."

"Will Captain Koeppler get him out for us, perhaps?" Helga inquired.

"Perhaps," Mutti said softly. "Meantime, Papa can write to us."

"From where?" Lilli demanded. "Where is he? Why can't your 'friend' have him sent home at once?"

"Don't be silly," Mutti flared. "The captain is not my 'friend.' He is only a classmate from the lower school, many years ago. It was good that he could tell us where Papa was taken. It's a camp for those who are awaiting trial, or for others having to be punished: Buchenwald."

The name meant little to the girls or even to Mutti. Later, they would learn that Buchenwald was the second of the many notorious labor and concentration camps to be built in Germany—a place of backbreaking toil, starvation and torture, and, almost always, death.

And what was the "good advice" that Mutti's former school friend had given her?

Lilli learned that, in the captain's words, it was to "leave this apartment, which is suspect because of your husband's activities. You will always be under surveillance here. You can save yourself and even your half-Jewish children by going back to your family home. "Surely,"

Captain Koeppler had concluded, "Frau and Herr Bayer, your highly respected parents, would not deny shelter to you and your young ones."

And so it had happened that Elspeth had gone off first to live with Oma and Opa Bayer, most of the Heinrichstrasse furniture was sold (even the grand, richly-carved bed of Oma and Opa Frankfurter), and Lilli and Helga found themselves attic-dwellers in the Bayer household.

Two

Even before the girls are out of bed, Gerda comes whirling into their "eagle's nest," as Lilli has sourly come to call it. The *Fuhrer,* or Nazi leader, as Adolph Hitler is called, has such a retreat in the form of a chalet on the top of an Alpine peak, where he holds secret conferences.

"Only *he's* up there to dominate the world," Lilli has remarked, "while our attic may as well be a dungeon."

What Lilli meant was how restricted their lives had become, hers and Helga's, because of the many anti-Jewish laws that either came into effect or were strengthened following *Kristallnacht* last November. Jews in Nazi Germany may no longer own radios or typewriters, travel on public transportation, go to the theater or the cinema, to parks or beaches, or to restaurants other than the few cafes still operated by Jews. They must carry ration books stamped with the letter *J,* limiting the kinds and quantities of food or other goods they may purchase, and can only live only in apartment blocks that bear the Star of David symbol and the letter *J* above the entrance. So, in effect, the girls are being hidden away in the Bayer household.

But there's little use reviewing these familiar obstacles this morning, as Gerda bustles around, clapping her hands and ordering "Up, up!" She is of uncertain age, gray-haired and dumpling-cheeked, with a body like that of a sturdy wooden doll. For Lilli and Helga, Gerda has come to be Grossmutter Bayer's daily emissary.

The girls never address the proud older lady with the informal "Oma" that they used with their wizened, loving Frankfurter grandma before her death. Nor do Lilli and Helga, although living under the roof of the same austere gray-stone house, see much of the elder Bayers, who keep Elspeth close to them in the lower quarters. Grossvater is a more cheerful-looking character than Grossmutter. He appears to be a jolly fellow of the old school and still wears side-whiskers. But he is always hurrying off on "official business," so the two older girls feel they hardly know him.

"You are to take special care with washing and dressing this morning," Gerda instructs. "You are going on a shopping outing with your grandmother. Everything must be immaculate. And you are to wear your best clothes."

Helga and Lilli are speechless. How can this be? It has never happened before. Grossmutter has lavished lots of care on Elspeth and has even shown her blonde little angel off to her women friends. But she has not taken Helga and Lilli anywhere since they have come to live with her, or even appeared to be very concerned with their secluded daily life.

True, she did engage a tutor for the two older girls, because Mutti is now working at a job in a fashion house (as she did before her marriage to Papa). So Mr. Anton Hess, with his sharp-tipped nose and *pince-nez* eyeglasses, comes every weekday to give Helga and Lilli instruction in science, history, and English. "Enough German grammar," Grossmutter decreed aloud soon after the girls moved in. *"Englisch!"*

Helga has never questioned this peculiarity. In view of the fact that England is declared to be Nazi Germany's chief target of destruction, why would Grossmutter Bayer want her granddaughters to learn English? "Perhaps," Lilli remarks slyly, "she is training us to be spies!"

Helga finds this "crazy," but Lilli insists it could be true. "Once we know English, the Hitler secret service will smuggle us into England to send them signals about the English war plans. But instead, while there, we could escape the Nazi clutches and become free."

"Yes," Helga mocks, "and send for Mutti and Elspeth, and get Papa out of Buchenwald, and live happily ever after. You read too many books, Lilli, all of them fairy tales!"

The mention of Papa returns Lilli to the somber mood that underlies her every conscious minute these days. Yes, there has been some mail from him. The first was a postcard, written from Buchenwald about three weeks after his arrest, which raised everyone's hopes. *My loved ones, I am fine and thinking of you only, as I wait for my case to be reviewed. You cannot write to me, but I will write you again. Do not worry. I send my love to you, Martina, and to my three treasured girls. Josef/Papa*

Hope began to fade, however, after a second and a third postcard arrived, bearing the same message in Papa's handwriting, but with a later date. What could this mean? Only last week a fourth post card of the same kind arrived. "It's as if Papa wrote these cards all at the same time, but dated them several weeks apart," Lilli had commented to Mutti. "Why would he do that?"

Mutti had shrugged sadly. "I will try to inquire," she murmured.

"From who? How?" Lilli challenged.

Mutti had turned away and reached for her handkerchief.

It is time for the trip to the *Kaufhaus*, the large and elaborate department store that is the pride of this medium-sized German city.

The façade of the store could be that of a palace, with many windows and carved stone decorations. It sits in the busiest part of downtown and has six stories and a basement that are served by electric elevators. Each mirrored and gilt-trimmed moving car is run by a uniformed young woman, who calls out the number of the floor and the type of merchandise offered for sale.

Lilli says she can remember having been to the *Kaufhaus* before, when she was four or five. She insists to Grossmutter in a friendly way that she has often seen this "dream palace" in her sleep. Helga says that can't be true, while Grossmutter remarks that Lilli has a "too-strong imagination." But Lilli remembers the ground-level floor, where they sell beauty accessories, ladies' gloves, handbags, silk stockings, and fine jewelry. She is certain now that she has been here with Mutti. Of course, she and her sister won't be lingering on this exotic ground floor—they are both too young for such frippery.

What are Lilli and Helga hoping for on this surprise shopping trip, on a sun-drenched May day that heralds warmer weather? They are visualizing cool summer frocks of cotton or linen, with short sleeves and a bit of smocking or embroidery, new underwear to replace their itchy winter garments, half-socks, and shoes with straps, not laces!

"Come along," Grossmutter urges, as the girls' heads are turned by smartly-dressed women shoppers, and even some gentlemen and high-ranking officers who are sniffing perfumes, holding jeweled earrings up to the light, and examining incredible alligator handbags.

Who would have thought, Lilli muses to herself, *that with all the rationing of everyday goods, such luxuries are still plentiful in Germany?*

Now at last they are in the miraculous elevator, smoothly passing the so-named "first floor" of the great emporium, which is devoted to men's apparel ranging from formal wear to shooting jackets, and includes hats, shoes, sleepwear and whatever other garments the man of wealth and standing might require.

Lilli's heart gives a thump as the elevator slows for the second floor, women's and girls' apparel. Other passengers file past them and leave the car, but Grossmutter restrains Helga and Lilli, who look up in puzzlement.

More floors flit past them . . . china, silverware, and home furnishings on the third; radios, gramophones, toys, and souvenirs on the fourth. Perhaps they are going directly to the lacy glass-roofed tea room and restaurant on the sixth floor, known as the Winter Garden. Dainty sandwiches, tiny iced cakes, and chocolate torte with whipped cream are its afternoon-tea specialties.

It is two hours later and the girls are back in their attic room, with Gerda helping them to sort out their new clothing. Lilli had been so close to the Winter Garden that she could almost taste its goodies, but had never reached the *Kaufhaus* pinnacle. Instead, Grossmutter had ushered them out of the elevator on the fifth floor, sports clothes and sporting goods for the entire family, and there they had made their purchases.

Then, at the very end of the shopping trip, Grossmutter Bayer had taken the girls down to the famed food court in the basement of the store. There, a tantalizing spectacle of gourmet specialties dazzled the girls' eyes. Smoked meats and sausages, cheeses, bakery delicacies of every sort, jams and preserves, and an array of chocolates and other confectionery, crammed the shelves. Small samples of some of the foods were offered to the roaming shoppers.

Lilli and Helga, hungry by this time, were permitted to help themselves to tiny squares of imported Norwegian goat cheese impaled on toothpicks. Helga gulped and spat the sweetish caramel-colored lump into her palm. Lilli managed to down hers, acknowledging that it was the most awful thing she had ever tasted. Grossmutter angrily muttered, "Manners!" and hurried both girls out of the *Kaufhaus*. It was the last time Lilli would ever lay eyes on the great store.

Without a word, Gerda clips the price tags from the girls' new clothing and neatly folds the drab-colored blouses, skirts, jackets, and high socks that are to be stored in the room's huge wooden wardrobe, presumably for summer wear. There are also new shoes, brown oxfords *with* laces, and high leather boots for each girl. The only really welcome item is the new cotton underwear that will replace the worn flannels of the seemingly endless winter.

"Such long faces," Gerda remarks. "What did you expect? Summer frocks? Parasols? Dancing shoes?"

Helga is silent, but Lilli speaks up. "We will look like Hitler Youth marchers in these clothes, but without the swastikas sewn onto them. Where can we go on sporting trips? What can we do with hiking boots when we never leave this house? Why has Elspeth been dressed up like a doll in frills and hairbows?"

Gerda lowers her head and shakes it from side to side. "You must speak to your Mutti. That is all I have to say." Then she disappears from the room.

Lilli has been lying awake for hours. Threads of various thoughts trail aimlessly through her head. It has been three days since the shopping trip and nothing has changed. In the silent, sleeping house, she hears a faint click, perhaps the turning of a key in a lock.

Mutti has been out this evening, as she often is lately, modeling the new fashions or perhaps attending a supper party. In the morning, she will be gone again. When will Lilli have a chance to speak with her?

Halfway down the dark stairway that ascends to the attic, there is a landing with a doorway to Gerda's room. Lilli creeps past on bare feet. It must be very late, perhaps two AM. She can hear the sound of Gerda's snoring and prays it will continue.

Now she has successfully reached the landing of the

second floor, where the elder Bayers, Mutti, and Elspeth have their quarters. She pauses there, wondering if Mutti has yet gone to her room, or is still on the main floor of the house.

As Lilli listens, she becomes aware of the deep, droning vibration of a male voice coming from the drawing room. She temporarily pulls back in shock, then continues creeping partway down the main staircase to give herself a view of the space below.

Sure enough, the voice is *his*, that of Captain Koeppler. He sits beside Mutti, who is dressed in glamorous evening wear, a white fur around her neck and silver, high-heeled, T-strap evening sandals on her slender feet.

Lilli listens to words that at first make no sense to her and are, at the same time, terrifying. "I am sorry, Martina, I know I promised both. But there is only room for one, and probably not until late summer."

Mutti murmurs a few words that are unclear. Lilli can tell she has been crying.

"The darker one," Koeppler replies. "She is the most endangered. Be reasonable. You will come through much better than most. There will always be that black mark against you . . . and them."

Mutti chokes back a sob. "Helga has not got the temperament for it. Even Elspeth would do better, spoiled as she now is. But I won't give up my littlest one. Never!"

There is movement now in the room below. The tall Nazi officer rises to his feet and pulls Mutti, limp and glittering, into his arms. Even at this horrifying moment, Lilli can't help admiring her mother's loveliness. She wears her thick pale-gold hair in a coiled bun at the base of her neck, exhibiting the beauty of her finely chiseled features.

Instantly, she pulls away from Koeppler and sighs deeply. Is the Captain just a helpful old school chum as Mutti has said, or is there something more between her and this hostile "friend?" Lilli is wracked with so much emotion that she fears she may cry out. Clapping her hand over her mouth, she turns and scampers rat-like up the stairs, past Gerda's room, and into her attic fortress.

It is the first time since Helga and Lilli have come to live with their Bayer grandparents that Gerda has informed them they are to descend to the small dining room for breakfast.

This news is amazing to Helga, even more so than the announcement of the recent shopping trip with Grossmutter. But to Lilli it is no surprise. Her swift retreat up the stairs from her hiding place in the wee hours of the morning had been detected in the drawing room after all. Mutti had followed her to her bedroom and tearfully explained that plans were being made for the safety of all three girls, plans which would be revealed in the morning.

Grossvater is seated at the table reading the morning paper. He is as cheerful as always, and he greets Helga and Lilli as though their presence at the family breakfast was an everyday affair. Grossmutter, who is solemnly pouring coffee, nods in a semi-friendly way and indicates where the girls are to sit. Mutti comes into the room, and Gerda is dismissed to take care of Elspeth, who isn't present.

Grossmutter places bowls of hot porridge before her granddaughters. Helga obediently digs in, but Lilli winces. Her breakfast choice is coffee and rolls. Mutti, who knows this, removes the porridge and sets bread and butter down before her. Grossmutter overlooks this and compliments Helga on her healthful choice of food.

Lilli glances at her yet-unknowing sister, for much has become clear to her during the many wakeful hours of the early morning. Something . . . she does not know what . . . has been planned for "the darker one," which would be Helga, who has Papa's olive-toned complexion, and his deep-brown eyes and hair. Lilli is fair, with gray-green eyes and honey-toned hair.

The innocent Helga finishes her porridge, and Grossmutter offers her breakfast cake and milky coffee, which she accepts politely. Lilli seethes. She knows that there are plans to send Helga away. Why doesn't somebody say something?

Then, as though has heard Lilli's inner plea, Grossmutter seats herself directly opposite eleven-year-old Helga and declares, "Grossvater and I have good news for you, my child. How would you like to travel to a good home in England, where you can hike, swim, and skate, go to school with other children, enjoy the cinema and other pleasurable outings? Wouldn't you like such an opportunity? It would be only until things are easier in Germany. Then you could return to us."

"Yes, my child," Grossvater chimes in, "you are lucky, for it has been arranged with the Jewish committee for the saving of the children that you are to have a place on the Kindertransport . . ."

Lilli jumps to her feet. She has heard vague talk of taking tens of thousands of Jewish children out of Nazi-occupied Europe by train and boat—from Germany, Austria, and Czechoslovakia—before Hitler's armies invade even more of the continent.

"Yes!" Lilli declares. "And I want to go, too. We must all go, Elspeth, too. Papa would want it that way. How can you think of separating us so cruelly?"

But no one is listening to her. All eyes are on Helga, who has dashed her coffee cup to the floor and run screaming from the breakfast room, "No, no never! Never will I be such a coward as to let myself be driven out of Germany. Never."

Three

It is the middle of the long, hot summer of 1939. Several months have passed since the anguished scene at the breakfast table in May, and there has been no further mention of sending Helga away on the Kindertransport.

Yet, everyone knows that the danger for Jews hiding in Germany is drawing closer every minute. And so, too, is war with England. The girls' tutor, Mr. Anton Hess, is their main source of information. He has told them that England is threatening to attack Germany if Hitler attempts to occupy one more country in Europe.

"Ah, but," says the all-knowing Mr. Hess, his *pince-nez* glasses flickering as he lowers and shakes his head in scholarly fashion, "the *Fuhrer* has already announced in May that Germany must have more *Lebensraum*, living space. He has vowed that he will have his armies in Poland by late summer."

The threat of war, as well as further actions against Jews everywhere, has started all sorts of rumors. Gerda has murmured tidbits to Helga and Lilli about the attic room no longer being a safe place in which to hide them from the Nazis, in spite of the Bayers' connections with members of the government.

"Where will they put us then?" Helga challenges.

Lilli looks at her sister anxiously. Helga has changed a great deal in the past months. She has become more assertive and outspoken.

Gerda tosses the girls fresh linens with which to make up their beds and replies as she leaves the room. "There is perhaps the coal bin."

Helga and Lilli stare at each other, wide-eyed. Then they do their room chores and, as usual, don the drab clothes that Grossmutter purchased for them in the spring. It's become obvious that their grandmother's intention was for the girls to be as incognito as possible, even inside the Bayer house.

But the onset of summer has allowed the two older Frankfurter girls one privilege—they are permitted to spend time in the grim, overgrown, walled garden that surrounds the large house. There, they pass the hours rereading English-language books, assigned to them by Mr. Hess, according to Grossmutter's orders. They skip rope, they toss a ball around, they even play hide and seek among the overgrown shrubs.

"This is stupid and childish," Helga exclaims one day. "I will not continue to be trapped in here like an animal." She walks away from Lilli, declaring that she is going to search for an escape hatch in the garden well. Lilli shakes her head in despair at Helga's foolishness and tries to concentrate on reading a peculiar English book called *Alice's Adventures in Wonderland.*

After a long while, Helga returns. She is flushed and perspiring, and her hands and knees match the dirt color of her khaki skirt and blouse. "I've found a place behind the shrubs," she reports excitedly, "where the wall is crumbling and the earth beneath it is soft."

Lilli jumps to her feet, letting the annoying *Alice* book fall to the ground. "You are out of your mind," she retorts. "What are you thinking? Even if you *could* make a space to wriggle through, where would you go?"

"Skating," Helga replies triumphantly. "Oh, Lilli, remember how we loved to skate before we were forced to wear the yellow stars. On the ice, in the park, such a wonderful feeling of flying away, of freedom! I wear no yellow star now. Who would know what I am? I could be just any child out for play."

Lilli grabs her sister's arm almost roughly. "Helga, come to your senses. Germany will soon be at war. It is already more dangerous than ever for a Jew in hiding to be discovered. You heard what Gerda said about the need to perhaps hide us in the coal bin. You could ruin everything—for Mutti, for Elspeth, even for the Bayers."

Helga shrugs off Lilli's arm. Nothing more is said that day about Helga's plan to slither out of their stronghold for a skating outing.

* * *

For the rest of the summer, Lilli keeps careful watch over her sister. When the two of them are in the garden during the oppressive days of August, trying to cope with its dankness and humidity, Lilli barely takes her eyes off Helga, who sulkily drags herself off to some distant perch with her schoolbag of reading assignments.

Sure enough, there comes an afternoon when Lilli looks up to where Helga was sitting. Her sister is nowhere in sight! Lilli quickly makes her way to the spot Helga had shown her, beneath the crumbling wall. The hole, now larger than when Lilli first saw it, shows signs of having recently been disturbed. Lilli, her heart pounding, contemplates following Helga out into the dangerous world of the open streets. But suppose she cannot find her sister and they are both discovered missing? Suppose they are both apprehended by the Hitler police and found to have no identity cards—an immediate sign that they are hidden Jews?

Lilli paces the area around the hole in the wall. Where is the schoolbag that Helga brought with her into the garden? Then, Helga's deception becomes clear to Lilli. The schoolbag did not contain books; it contained Helga's roller skates.

Anguished minutes go by and add up to nearly three-fourths of an hour. Gerda may appear at any moment to call the girls indoors. What will Lilli tell her? How far can they trust Grossmutter's loyal servant, whose true feelings toward them have always been a mystery?

Lilli tracks the garden restlessly, returning every few minutes to examine the hole in hope of Helga's return. She is at the point of despair when she hears a rustling in the shrubbery behind her and there, rising from a crouch to her full height, is Helga, her skates in one hand and her empty schoolbag in the other. Her dark eyes are flashing, and she wears a challenging smile. A single tear of bright red blood descends from a cut high up on her forehead.

Lilli dashes forward. "What have you done? Oh, Helga . . ."

Helga touches her forehead lightly, glances at her reddened, glistening finger, and continues to smile. "No, Lilli, it's not what you think. No one threw stones at me. The other children did not chase me. I fell, that was all. The skating path was not so smooth."

But Lilli knows better. Last year, she and Helga were stoned several times by the Hitler Youth, at the ice rink, in the park, on their bicycles. They would seek out new places, but their enemies would always discover them. Eventually, they were forced to remain indoors.

Lilli hurries Helga silently toward the house. They stumble up the back stairs to the bathroom, where they wash Helga's cut and compress it to stop the bleeding. Lilli puts a plaster on the wound and Helga combs her thick dark hair on a slant across her forehead. The two of them gaze into the mirror. In spite of her anguish, Lilli bursts out laughing. "Do you know who you look like? Ah, if only you had a moustache!"

It is August 27, 1939. Mr. Hess has arrived to give Helga and Lilli their morning lesson. The tutor is in a jubilant mood. He struts around the room with his hands behind his back, exclaiming, "Today the *Fuhrer* has demanded Poland's port to the sea, as well, of course, the rest of the country. The Polish army, such as it is," he sniffs, "is mobilizing. And Britain is ready to declare war on Germany. "Young ladies," he adds, "you are about to see history being made."

Lilli, who has on occasion mocked the stuffy Mr. Hess behind his back, declares, "What is so wonderful about going to war? Everyone will suffer, even the Germans."

Helga backs Lilli up with a sarcastic remark. "When Hitler goes into Poland he will find many more Jews to kill. That will give him even more *Lebensraum*."

Mr. Hess looks a bit flustered. He's been teaching these half-Jewish students because he needed the work, and the Bayers convinced him his undertaking would be kept secret. Before he can respond to the challenges of his too-well-taught students, there is a rapid knocking at the door, and Mutti enters the room, with Gerda directly behind her.

Lilli and Helga are instantly alarmed, and Mr. Hess seems a bit taken aback, too. It's most unusual for Mutti to visit the girls during the day. Her expression is sad, though she is smiling.

"The papers have come for you, my Helga dear." she says softly. Mutti is holding up some official-looking documents. "Your passport has been approved, and there is no time to lose. The next Kindertransport is to leave for England on September 1st. In just a few days. If war breaks out, heaven spare us, this train may be the last to reach safety. Gerda will help you pack the things you must take with ..."

Mutti never finishes her sentence. Helga, once the most obedient of the three Frankfurter sisters, hurls herself at Mutti, screaming furiously. *I told you I would never go. I refuse to give in to their threats and persecutions. I am not a mouse to be chased away with a broom.*

Mutti brushes a tear from her cheek. "Be sensible, my child. You are one of the fortunate ones. There is room for only a limited number of children on this final transport. You must not give up your chance for freedom."

Lilli turns her back and walks to the window. She gazes down at the street below, which is almost deserted in the summer heat. She's never told Helga what she overheard the night she spied on Mutti and Captain Koeppler. Tears spring to her eyes. Perhaps she and Helga have not been the closest of sisters, despite being only one year apart in age. Still, they have grown up together, and experienced the increasing harshness of the Nazi offensive against Jews. And, although they try never to speak of it, they are both almost certain they've lost Papa to the brutalities of the Buchenwald concentration camp. The mysterious postcards, with staggered dates but the same bland message, have long ceased to arrive. And Mr. Hess has whispered rumors of prisoners being worked to death in the harsh Buchenwald stone quarries. *"You must fight such hatred all your lives,"* Papa said upon being arrested on *Kristallnacht*. What, Lilli ponders, is the best way to do that?

She turns away from the window. This is what she will tell Helga. *It is, after all, what Papa would have wanted . . .*

But Helga is nowhere in sight. Mutti has collapsed onto the bed and is sobbing uncontrollably. Gerda is bustling out the door, calling after Helga in German, *"Halt, Halt!"* Mr. Hess is rapidly gathering up his teaching materials, preparing to make a swift exit.

Lilli is much fleeter than the chunky-bodied Gerda, and easily slips past her on the staircase and races into the garden, just in time to see Helga disappear behind the untidy shrubs that conceal the hole beneath the crumbling wall. This time Lilli doesn't hesitate. She dives crazily into the loose earth, wriggles through the opening, staggers to her feet on the deserted street, and chases after Helga.

Both girls have always been fast runners, winning races even back when they were quite small and attended the German school. But today Lilli fears she will never catch her sister, who is sprinting ahead. She musn't lose sight of Helga, whose drab clothing could easily help her to vanish into the crowd on the next street, where a trolley line runs and there are shops rather than large houses surrounded by garden walls.

Where can Helga be going? Does *she* even know? Doesn't she see the danger of attracting attention? Lilli has a vision of Helga causing a scuffle in the street and being arrested by the Nazi police, who will take her to headquarters. There, she will be forced to reveal the hideout of her half-Jewish sisters. Mutti and the Bayers will be found guilty, and they will all be swallowed up into one of the concentration camps.

These images push Lilli to pursue Helga with a renewed burst of energy. The busy traffic street at the corner is already in sight, and Lilli has very little time to pounce on the fleeing Helga and bring her to the ground. She imagines herself a cheetah, an animal she saw once on a visit to the zoo, said to be the fastest land animal on earth. She wills herself to give all she has to the chase.

The distance between the sisters begins to shrink. Lilli is getting closer and closer. Finally, with one fierce effort, she hurls her body into the air, thrusts her right arm as far ahead of her as she can, and catches the sleeve of Helga's blouse.

There is a loud thud, followed by a cracking sound that sends a wave of sickness through Lilli's body. Her stilled prey lies before her, moaning in pain.

Four

True to his promise, on September 1, 1939, Adolf Hitler sends Nazi Germany's fiercest fighting divisions into neighboring Poland. True to *their* promise, the governments of Great Britain and France declare war on Germany two days later. World War II has begun.

The morning of September 1 finds Lilli and Mutti on the busy street with the trolley line, on the very block where Lilli tackled Helga to the ground just a few days before. Mutti, always much more stylishly dressed than the average German *Frau*, wears a flowered-chiffon summer dress and a brimmed straw hat, tilted at a charming angle.

Lilli, already tall for her age, walks beside her mother. She is dressed in her usual khaki clothing, high socks, and sturdy shoes. She carries both a small suitcase and a backpack. Her heart is racing. She could never have imagined this scene until the day of Helga's accident . . . Helga, who now rests with her broken arm and dislocated shoulder in a cast, attended in the attic room by Gerda and a hired nurse.

After Helga's fall, people began to gather, seemingly from nowhere, muttering and making suggestions for lifting her from the ground. Several older men and women scolded Lilli for having knocked her sister down. The police were sure to be arriving at any minute to investigate the hubbub.

It was Gerda who saved the day, huffing and puffing as she caught up with the runaway and her pursuer. With great strength and care, she lifted Helga to her feet, carefully embraced her wounded arm and shoulder, and walked her back to the house, with Lilli trailing shamefacedly behind.

"Just a bit of roughhousing," Gerda soothed the slowly-dispersing crowd. "They are sisters and members of the Hitler Youth."

The harried days that followed were taken up with Mutti's daring plan to have Lilli substitute for Helga on the Kindertransport.

"How can this happen?" Lilli asked her mother. "I am a year older and Helga and I don't look alike. They will not honor the passport. And what will happen to Helga, and to the rest who remain behind?" Lilli insisted that she was cheating Helga of a chance for freedom that was rightfully hers.

Mutti was gentle but persuasive. "You wanted to go from the very start, Lilli. How foolish to waste this chance for freedom. Once you are in England, you may be able to save us all." With that, Mutti pressed into Lilli's hand the name and address of Papa's brother, Herman, who lived in America. Lilli remembered hearing her parents speak of the American relatives, with whom Papa had corresponded for years prior to his arrest. Herrman knew of their plight, but had been unable to help the family because of his country's strict immigration laws. So, for Lilli, the Kindertransport would be more than just an escape from Nazi Germany—it would also be a mission to find a way to contact her uncle.

Before her departure, Lilli tried to make peace with her sister. "What are you so worried about, Lilli?" Helga remarked cynically. "You know I didn't want to be sent away like a scared bunny. I'll stay here and fight for my rights."

"What rights?" Lilli exclaimed. "You haven't any here in Germany. Where were you even running that day? Into the arms of the street police, or those brutes, the Brown Shirts, or straight to the Gestapo itself?"

Helga turned away, gingerly lifting her right arm and shoulder in their hard cast.

"We won't talk about it anymore," she pronounced.

The trolley is crowded and noisy, and there is an air of excitement everywhere. All along the route, groups of Hitler Youth are marching through the streets, cheering and carrying flags and large banners bearing swastikas.

The news of the *Fuhrer's* invasion of Poland has traveled fast, and the German people appear to be supporting him in his reckless grab for conquest and power.

Mutti and Lilli sit rigidly side by side and do not speak until Mutti announces, "We will get off at the next stop."

Lilli peers out the window. They are still a few blocks away from the bustling railroad station. Mutti explains that it will be better to say goodbye at some distance from the train platform, as the Nazi authorities frown on too much public display.

Mother and daughter descend from the trolley and make their way through the congested streets. Lilli has already said goodbye to her Bayer grandparents and little Elspeth, as well as to Helga, the two sisters crying and hugging each other. Soon it will be time to say goodbye to Mutti, who remains a mystery to Lilli. Noting the presence of so many Hitler police and high-level Nazi officers surrounding the railroad station, Lilli thinks about the tall shadowy figure of Captain Koeppler. What is his true relationship to Mutti? Was Papa betrayed by Mutti's "old school friend" or has he been helped? If Papa is alive, why can't the Captain get word to them from him?

"I will write to you, Lilli my child," Mutti says as they drawer closer to the station. "And you will write to me. We must never lose touch . . ."

"And you will let me know the first thing if you hear

from Papa," Lilli interrupts. "And tell me about Helga and Elspeth ..."

Their words are drowned out by the noise of blaring announcements, harsh commands, and the shrillness of the train whistle. A moment later, mother and daughter are being wedged apart by the steely shoulders of the uniformed police. They manage one last embrace before Lilli is swept away in the direction of the nearest railroad car.

The Nazi guards shove the children onto the train like so many cattle. Toddlers are carried aboard by older children, and there are even some infants in the arms of brother and sisters, themselves no more than teenagers. No parents or guardians are allowed to go along. The only adults on the train will be the German officers.

Lilli reaches a seat beside a window in the dreary car, which quickly fills up and overflows into the next car and the next. There are perhaps two hundred children about to travel on what will likely be the last Kindertransport ever to leave Germany.

Lilli peers out the window, trying to get one more view of Mutti. She manages to catch a glimpse of her mother's tall, lovely figure in the crush on the station platform.

But with so many little faces pressed against the grimy windows, Mutti doesn't see Lilli, who is waving furiously amid the clutter and tears of her fellow children. Soon only a tiny space remains in the window, through which Lilli catches a final view of Mutti, dabbing her eyes with a handkerchief. Beside her, stands the tall, grim figure of Captain Gerhardt Koeppler.

It's almost a relief for Lilli to look away from the window into the stern face of one of the German soldiers, who are checking for name tags and luggage identification. The tags mean that the children have valid travel visas, or passports. Any child without a tag will be removed from the train.

Lilli gropes nervously for her visa. It is there, pinned to her coat. Then she is asked to point out her luggage. The officer lifts up her backpack and suitcase, and seems to be weighing them. He hefts the backpack questioningly. "What have you got in there?" he asks with a grin, "the family silver?"

Alarmed, Lilli gulps. "Books. Some English books to read."

The soldier's grin widens into a toothy smile as he presses the pack to feel its contents and then sets it down beside Lilli. "Ha. Well, good luck to you then, Helga Frankfurter." And he is gone.

Helga! She is now Helga. Lilli must never forget this. She will be Helga forever. And who will Helga be? What will become of her?

Lilli is still pondering this awful question when she feels a jolt and realizes that the train is leaving the station. Soon they will be clattering through the countryside on their way to the border with Holland, where they will at last be beyond the clutches of German authority.

The seats in the train are arranged to face each other, so that some of the children are riding forward, and some backward. From her cramped position beside the window, Lilli looks directly across into the eyes of a bespectacled boy who, unlike many of the others, is well-dressed for the journey. He is so proper and neat that she can't help smiling at him and, to her surprise, he smiles back and thrusts out his hand.

"Stefan Korzak," he announces with formal courtesy. Lilli imagines that if he was on his feet he would click his heels.

"Li . . . Helga Frankfurter," she replies, stumbling a bit. "Where are you from?"

Lilli learns that Stefan is from a Jewish family in Austria. The country has been under Nazi rule since March 1938, so his parents have arranged for him to live with the family of his uncle, a businessman in England.

"What about you?" he asks Lilli.

Lilli hunches her shoulders. "I don't know where I will live. But I do have an uncle in America. Perhaps I can go to live with him some day."

Stefan leans forward, his eyeglasses glinting in the staggered light of the rumbling train. "Don't plan on it. They don't let Jews in that easily."

Lilli feels for Herman Frankfurter's address, which

is sewn into the pocket of her blouse, and shudders. She doesn't want to talk to Stefan Korzak anymore. He is surely one of the very lucky members of the Kindertransport, clean, and well-dressed.

Babies, in the arms of children Lilli's age, cry incessantly. Every now and then the smell of vomit wafts through the car. Some of the young travelers have motion sickness; others are frightened. Gerda has packed a lunch for Lilli of bread and cheese and fruit. But her stomach is turning and she wants nothing to eat. She leans back against the hard wooden seat and shuts her eyes. But images leap before her . . . her goodbyes to Helga and Elspeth, the barking orders and rough handling of the Nazi guards at the railroad station, her last glimpse of Mutti with the menacing Captain Koeppler at her side . . .

Lilli is awakened by the sharp, jerky movements of the slowing train, and by the sound of cheering coming from within the railroad car. Stefan Korzak is leaning toward her with a gleaming smile. "We have come to the Dutch border," he announces. "We are free, Helga Frankfurter. Free!"

Lilli rubs her eyes. She is being crushed by her seat-mates, who have swarmed to the windows, seeking their first view of Holland, a free country (even though the *Fuhrer* has already made plans to swallow it up, along with Belgium and even France).

Stefan, who has a better view of the Dutch railroad station from his window, informs Lilli that "the Nazi guards are leaving the train. And the Dutch train conductors are coming aboard. Goodbye to Hitler!"

There is more cheering, not only for the unarmed, blue-garbed trainmen entering the cars, but also for the many Dutch women and children who have come to see the Kindertransport pass through on its way to the seaport. Train windows have been opened and the kindly visitors are passing sandwiches and chocolate bars, even cups of hot cocoa, to the clamoring hands within. Lilli finds herself gulping back tears of surprise as a chocolate bar wrapped in gold paper is thrust into her hands

Too quickly, however, the train sounds its whistle, warning of its imminent departure for the ferry slips on the North Sea. "Goodbye!" the visitors cry out as they slowly disperse. "Good luck to you for a safe landing in England."

It's late in the day when the weary and sea-sickened Kindertransport travelers arrive in the English port of Harwich. They are taken to the assignment center, where they will meet their hosts. The children, so happy and refreshed during their brief stop in Holland, are now limp, and many of the little ones have fallen fast asleep. Even Stefan Korzak looks a bit roughed up despite his fine clothing. He suffered a sick stomach several times during the crossing, and Lilli couldn't help feeling sorry for him. But when his uncle and other family members come to claim him—and he and "Helga" exchange formal farewells—Lilli becomes envious again.

She has been sitting on a bench in the assignment center for what feels like a very long time. Little by little her younger companions have been offered homes, their luggage collected as they have gone off to live with their new families. But Lilli, who appears older than her twelve years, is repeatedly passed over. *What if nobody wants me?* she worries. *I've come so far. Mutti said I would be safe here, but where will I live?*

Her thoughts are interrupted by one of the refugee officers overseeing the welfare of the diminishing number of Kindertransport arrrivals. "Not to worry, dear," says the pleasant-voiced woman. "I promise you'll have a bed tonight and a warm meal."

"But where?" Lilli asks anxiously. An Army transport has arrived to take several of the oldest refugee boys and girls to an orphanage. Lilli is not sure what a British orphanage is like, but it does not sound like the "good home in England" that Grossmutter Bayer had described. "I want to live some place where I can go to school and . . . and skate and do sports, and go to the cinema . . ."

"Of course, of course, all in good time," the officer

assures her in a friendly manner. "But meanwhile, dear, we must assure that your basic needs are taken care of. Please collect your things and come with me."

With a sinking heart, Lilli slings her backpack over her shoulders, picks up her suitcase, and haltingly approaches the waiting transport.

Five

The daylight hours of an English summer seem to go on and on. It is still bright out as Lilli bounces along on a country road in a battered farm truck, seated between her new family, a Mr. and Mrs. Rathbone, instead of in the Army transport that was to have taken her to the orphanage.

She was about to climb into the transport with the other older children who had not been claimed when she felt a tap on her shoulder. "There are some people here asking about you," said the refugee officer. "Come and speak to them."

Mrs. Rathbone, whose first name is Agnes, is tall and thin-lipped, with black hair that is scraped back from her face and gathered into a tight knot. She did most of the talking, while her stout, gray-bearded husband, Wilfred, stared silently at Lilli through small, watery eyes.

"You're a tall one. Have you already finished school?"

"*Nein*," Lilli hastened to reply, adding in English that she wanted to go to school to learn to read and write the language.

"Ah, but you already understand it," answered the canny Mrs. Rathbone. "There's a school for the young ones in the village, if they'll take you. As for your new home, we've a poultry farm in the countryside with lots to keep you busy. Life there is a bit old-fashioned but it's a healthy place and you'll be safe from the bombs Hitler is sure to drop on our towns and cities."

When the refugee officer asked if she accepted the offer to go and live with the Rathbones, Lilli readily answered, "Yes," in English. Her belongings were removed from the Army truck and tossed into the open back of the Rathbones' farm vehicle, which was filled with straw, chicken feathers, and numerous egg crates.

Twilight is beginning to descend when Mr. Rathbone drives off the unpaved road, lined with hedgerows, into an even narrower one. Soon the farmhouse and its surroundings come into view. At first, the snuggling house, built of rough stone and topped by a roof of thatch, reminds Lilli of pictures in the German storybooks she read when she was small. For Lilli, who has lived in a city all her life, the image of a country cottage has always been a romantic one. So she is startled when she steps from the truck into a slab of thick mud, toward which chickens come running from all directions, accompanied by the barking of two large dogs. For a moment, Lilli wonders if, like *Alice* in the book she has been reading, she has fallen into a rabbit hole.

"That'll teach you, my lady," says the burly Mr. Rathbone with a basso laugh. "Have you never been on a farm before?" Mrs. Rathbone doesn't wait for an answer, hurrying Lilli—who struggles to retrieve her suitcase and backpack from the truck—along impatiently. "It's already late for tea, and we'll have an early night for certain," Mrs. Rathbone mutters seemingly to herself.

Lilli follows her hostess out of the filthy yard and up a pathway of half-sunken paving stones to the farmhouse entrance. Framed in the doorway stands a small, roly-poly boy, with the broad Mongolian features of a child born with a defect. He appears to have been crying, his knotted fists still rubbing at his eyes. But he lights up at the sight of Mrs. Rathbone, reaching to grasp her about the hips.

"Have you been a good little son while we were away?" asks Mrs. Rathbone, already rushing past him to get the "tea" ready. "Look, Tim," she points to Lilli, "we've brought you a sister."

Lilli learns that the Rathbones' farmhouse, with its stone floors and tiny windows, has no electricity or running water. It is also revealed to her—thankfully—that "tea" in working-class England can also mean supper. She has been terribly hungry for a long time now.

Sitting at the rough wooden table in the kitchen that is also part sitting room, Lilli partakes with Tim and the

Rathbones of bread, cheese, pickles, and scalding cups of strong dark tea. She is offered sugar lumps but warned that, with the war on, she must restrict herself to no more than two.

Tim sits across from Lilli on the wooden bench, his huge, nearly black eyes boring into her.

"Now, mind your manners," Mrs. Rathbone cautions, as bits of moist chewed bread dribble from Tim's mouth. Lilli can see that he has trouble controlling his slobbering. He is also extraordinarily excited by the presence of this tall, graceful young girl, with gray-green eyes and tawny hair. When Lilli smiles at him, he giggles back and wriggles with happiness.

"Tim's a good boy, he is," Mrs. Rathbone assures her. "He's ten years old and a bit mischievous, but he means no harm."

Lilli asks if Tim goes to school.

"Learning's not for the likes of him," Mr. Rathbone growls. Lilli is struck by the harsh tone and the note of dismissal in Tim's father's voice.

When they are finished eating, Lilli climbs up the ladder to her room, which is in the loft under the eaves. Suddenly, the sadness she's been trying to repress overwhelms her. The moment she gets into bed, the sounds of small skittering creatures all around her in the dark, she begins to weep uncontrollably. She is crying for

Helga, for Elspeth, for Papa, for Mutti. She knows that, although she is out of the grasp of the mad *Fuhrer*, her loved ones are not. She would give anything to leave this strange place and take her chances hiding with the others in the coal bin of the Bayer house in Germany.

Lilli's life with the Rathbones quickly falls into a pattern. In the mornings, she wakes up early to feed the chickens before walking three miles to the local primary school. The students there are from the surrounding countryside, and Lilli is placed in a grade where no one is older than nine. Lilli, at age twelve, feels idiotic sitting at the back of the room, trying to learn as much English as she can while the class drones on doing multiplication tables and memorizing the names and dates of the monarchs of Great Britain.

When she inquires about attending a higher-level school, Mrs. Rathbone tells her that most advanced schools in England require fees. "Surely you can't expect us to manage that, Helga my dear," she says. "The funds we receive from the refugee committee barely cover your keep as it is."

Lilli frequently dwells on this as she does her daily after-school chores, sweeping and scrubbing the stone floor, gathering eggs, cleaning out the chicken coops, as well as looking after Tim. The last thing is something she cannot avoid, as he often comes into her room without invitation, wrapping his short, thick body around her with rough affection. He even walks to school with her and waits outside, peering in through the windows to the amusement of her schoolmates, until the teacher drives him away.

A few weeks after her arrival, Lilli writes her first letter to Mutti—in German, of course—trying to explain her new life.

"I find it very strange," she writes, "that people in the English countryside are so poor. They do not own their farms; they rent them from some great landowner who lives in a castle and rules over the entire domain. They must pay him from their earnings or they will be driven off the land."

"What odd foods we eat, especially for 'tea,' which is supper. Mainly, there is dried salty fish and boiled eggs, because we have plenty of those. There is no running water or indoor toilet, as we had on Heinrichstrasse and with the Bayers. The outhouse is full of spiders. And now that the weather has begun to turn cold at night, the chamber pots in the cottage have begun to freeze, for there is only the fireplace for heat. When I climb up to my bed in the loft, I take a heated brick or a large stone, wrapped in layers of flannel."

Lilli also tells Mutti about her grimly silent hosts, and about Tim. "I don't think they are mean people, but they are very sad and disappointed by their sick little boy.

I disagree with Tim's father. Tim should go to school and he should have friends. Sometimes I give him a few lessons. He is not stupid."

Lilli tries to keep her letter as factual as possible. She does not tell Mutti how heavy her heart is, with an ache that never goes away. She ends the letter hoping the family is still safe at the Bayers, and imploring Mutti to write back soon. But who knows what is happening now in wartime Germany?

It is now January 1940, and the English winter, with its bleak skies and chilling rains, has set in. Nonetheless, Lilli and Tim are venturing forth on a walk to the village, which Tim dearly loves to do. Lilli is focused on the small country post office, where she has been hoping for months to receive an answer to her letter to Mutti.

Tim is pointing as they tread along to the distant "castle" where the rich landowners of the estate live. It is the largest house Lilli has ever seen, four stories high and topped with numerous turrets and spires that appear to challenge the sky.

"Have you ever been inside the manor house?" Lilli asks Tim.

He shakes his head violently. "No. Mustn't never go there."

Lilli tries to imagine what it must be like inside: high ceilings, fireplaces and heating stoves in every room, elegant furnishings and draperies, and servants to look to one's every need. Could anything be more different than the chill and spare life at the Rathbones?

The soggy unpaved road on which Lilli and Tim have been navigating the puddles gives way to a hard surface as they approach the village, with its parish church, its pub, its inviting shops, and, of course, its post office.

As they are about to enter the main street, they come face to face with two little girls, who are, strangely, dressed in what Lilli would call "city clothes." They are bundled up against the cold in woolen coats and matching bonnets. Yet their knees are bare, and their shoes seem hardly suitable for country roads. Lilli, who is happy to see new faces, greets them with a smile. "You look like sisters," she can't refrain from remarking.

"Yes, we are. I'm Clarissa and this is Mabel," says the older of the two, who looks about ten. "We're from London. Where are you from? And what's the matter with him?" Tim clutches Lilli's hand more tightly.

So many nosy questions, Lilli thinks indignantly. "Nothing at all is the matter with him," she replies, and she promptly asks a nosy question of her own. "If you live in London, what are you doing here in the countryside?"

"Oh, we're Pied Piper children," Clarissa declares. "We've come to stay at the manor house until the Jerries stop blitzing London. There are four of us here now and more coming soon." Since the war began, there had been talk of a Blitz, an all-out bombing of British cities and towns by the terrifying *Luftwaffe*, the German air force. So the government organized the Pied Piper Operation, where British children are evacuated by bus or train to the countryside, where they will be out of harm's way.

Lilli can't help feeling jealous at the luck of the two sisters. Imagine if something so fortunate had happened to her and Helga. "What's it like there?" she inquires almost timidly.

"Ooh," Mabel speaks up for the first time. Lilli guesses she's around seven. "It's lovely. We've nothing so posh at home, our own rooms and a cook and a server for meals. We're even allowed to ride the horses. Today, we've come into the village in the van. My lady is going to outfit us with proper country clothing and allow us to buy sweeties."

Clarissa gives her little sister a sharp look. Perhaps Mabel is talking too much.

She narrows her eyes and says to Lilli. "You have an odd way of speaking. You're not English, are you?"

Lilli shakes her head. "I'm a refugee from Germany. I'm living now with a farm family in the nearby countryside. Tim here is their son."

Clarissa nods, but still seems a bit confused. She looks down at Lilli's boots, the same ones Grossmutter bought her at the *Kaufhaus* last spring. They are encrusted with farm filth, and the seams have begun to split. "You should get a new pair of those while you're in town," she says.

Angry tears spring to Lilli's eyes. She tugs hard at Tim's hand, and whirls him around in the direction of the village post office, walled with gray stone. *Why have I come here?* Lilli agonizes. *These people are strangers. Everywhere there are strangers!*

Six

"*My Beloved Child,*" Mutti writes in her fine slanted hand, "*We are in Amsterdam!*"

Lilli is so excited at having received her very first letter from Mutti that she hasn't even taken notice of the postmark and the unfamiliar stamp. She is sitting with Tim on the low stone wall that skirts the village post office. Tim is restless, kicking his short, solid legs against the wall. He has been begging for "sweeties" ever since the little Pied Piper girl, Mabel, mentioned them. "Yes, yes, Tim," Lilli promises. "I have only a little money but we will go to the sweet shop as soon as I read my letter." She shows him the single sheet of paper that she has withdrawn from the thin blue envelope, even though the writing is in German and, in any case, Tim has not been taught to read.

There is more good news from Mutti. "*I have with me, thanks to God, your sisters Elspeth and Helga. This move came about through your grandparents, who could no longer keep us with them.*" Mutti, however, offers no details as to why or how the family left the Bayers. "*It was most*

*fortunate that I received your letter before leaving Germany.
Even though the ways of your host family are strange to you,
be grateful that you have reached a place of safety. I trust that
you have written to your uncle in America. He is the only
hope for us to survive."*

As instructed, Lilli wrote to Papa's brother in
America as soon as she could after coming to stay with
the Rathbones. But four months have passed and there
has been no answer. She promises herself that she will
write to her uncle again immediately.

*"For now, Lilli, you must write to me at the address
below. Kind people here have taken us to live with them
for a while, so that I can work and earn some money, and
your sisters can go to school. But, as you may know, Hitler
is determined to invade Holland. Already there is a Dutch
Nazi party here. What will happen to us then, I do not know.
Sadly, there has been no word from Papa for a very, very
long time. Your sisters and your Mutti send you their deepest
felt love."*

"Why are you crying?" Tim asks Lilli as she carefully
refolds the nearly transparent sheet of paper and puts
it back into the envelope. The letter is dated December,
1939, and Lilli wonders how long will it be before the
Jews living in Holland have yellow stars sewn onto their
garments? She tries to stem her tears with her fingertips.
"Come," she says to Tim. "You've been very patient." She
helps him to get his thick body down from the wall. "I'll

buy you some sweeties. What kind do you think you will like?"

It is early April, and the English countryside is greening and flowering shrubs are in bloom. Lilli goes to school every day, hoping that her English will improve enough for her to be advanced to grade six, the highest in the primary school. As it is, she is still in grade four.

She often sees Clarissa and Mabel, surrounded by other Pied Piper children who are now living with them up at the manor house. Even ten-year-old Clarissa is in a higher grade than Lilli.

One day, Clarissa and some of her classmates approach Lilli as she is leaving school with Tim, who has come to walk home with her. The little girls are fascinated with him. "Can he talk?" one of them asks.

"Of course, he can," Lilli retorts stiffly. "He's just shy, especially when people keep staring at him."

"Will he ever grow up?" one of the other girls wants to know.

Lilli doesn't answer. She takes Tim's hand and they start to walk home. But the girls, who have now been joined by a few boys, follow them, calling out, "Tim, oh Tim, why won't you talk to us? Do you have a funny accent like Lilli?"

Lilli turns indignantly to face the group that has been teasing her and Tim.

"Why did you run away from Germany?" a friend of Clarissa's asks her. "It's because you're Jewish, isn't it?"

A great flush of anger and fear washes over Lilli. She turns from the children and tries to hurry Tim along. But he can't walk very fast on his short legs. Suddenly, Lilli feels a spray of pebbles on her back. Tim must have been hit, too, because he has stopped walking and is bending down to pick up pebbles to toss back. "No, no, Tim," Lilli cautions. He likes to throw pebbles at the chickens at home, so he probably thinks this is a game. And, of course, he would love to have friends to play with. However, Lilli is aware that the children are intent on playing a game of their own.

Lilli is bending down, prying a pebble out of Tim's hand, when the children start to chant something. At first, Lilli isn't sure what they are saying, but then the shouted words become clear to her. "*The idiot and the Jew, get off with you! No one wants you here. Get off with you.*" Tim doesn't understand the chant. He simply wants the game to continue. He picks up another stone, and throws it—surprisingly well—hitting an older boy on his bare leg.

Tim is now laughing gleefully, and Lilli can't hold onto him. Armed with yet another missile, he runs toward the enemy, only to fall down and receive a swift return blow to his forehead from a sharp-edged bit of rock. He lies in the road, bleeding heavily.

Lilli kneels down in horror. She rips off Tim's shirt and binds his head as tightly as she can to stem the flow of blood. When she looks up, the children have vanished. All she can see is a patch of country road littered with pebbles and small rocks.

Lilli and Tim are picked up by a passing motorist, who drops then off at the farm. Tim is crying and writhing about as Lilli helps to carry him into the house and place him on the sitting room couch.

Mrs. Rathbone runs into the room. "You wicked girl!" she shrieks at Lilli. She bends down over her son and unwraps the improvised bandage. "What have you done to him?"

"It was the children at school," Lilli tries to explain as she rushes around gathering water and cloths with which to cleanse Tim's wound. "They attacked us for no reason. Stoned us. Called us *the . . . the . . .* "

But Mrs. Rathbone isn't paying attention. She shoves Lilli aside, snatches her offerings, and gently bathes her little boy's forehead. Lilli is relieved to see that the wound is not as bad as it first appeared. There is a fairly large bruise and some torn flesh, but the bleeding is lessening.

"There now, there now," Mrs. Rathbone murmurs as she strokes Tim's hair. Lilli has seldom seen her act so tenderly with Tim. Suddenly, she looks up sharply at Lilli. "Now, tell me, girl, how did this happen?"

Lilli's lips cannot bear to form the word that was directed at Tim . . . *idiot*. "It was because of me," she replies. "They called me a *Jew*. They kept repeating, '*Jew, Jew, get off with you. No one wants you here.*' Then they started tossing pebbles at us, and then rocks. The bigger boys joined in with the girls who started it."

Tim is trying to say something about his having thrown a rock at a big boy, but his mother shushes him. She tells him she will bring him some tea and a biscuit and that he should rest quietly on the couch.

Lilli goes into the kitchen to put the kettle on. Mrs. Rathbone follows her. "Tim won't *ever* be following you to school anymore," she says. "And I think you know why."

"Yes," Lilli replies quietly.

"Which means *you* won't be going to school either," says Mrs. Rathbone, crossing her arms and pursing her thin lips. "There's plenty for you to do around here, and you can keep a watch on Tim as well . . ."

Lilli breaks in. "It doesn't matter. I don't *want* to go back there anyway. There's nothing important they can teach me in a class with nine-year-olds."

"Ah, now," Mrs. Rathbone remarks in a softer tone, "There's a bit of sense."

Due to the outbreak of war, butter, sugar, and meat are being rationed, and farmers are being encouraged to grow winter vegetables such as cabbage, turnips, and beets, as well as lettuce and other greens, in the summer.

Lilli is put to work helping Mr. Rathbone dig planting beds. "Now, now, my girl, you've got to put a bit more muscle into it," he comments, hovering her as she bends her slim body toward the ground. Lilli's hair has grown long, so she wears it braided and pinned up to keep it out of her eyes. She has never dug a garden before, and her palms have begun to blister. She is also very uncomfortable under Mr. Rathbone's wet gaze.

"Soon the rabbits will be arriving, m'girl," he tells her cheerfully. "They won't give you blisters and a sore back. You'll like tending 'em, right enough." Lilli has already been told that the Rathbones will be extending their poultry farm to raise rabbits for meat, and are even going to acquire a goat for milk that they can sell at the market. "But no pigs," Mr. Rathbone declares at tea that evening. "I won't have a pig, Agnes, say what you will. I know we can feed 'em kitchen waste, but who's going to do the butchering? Not me, ma'am."

At night, after working all day in the fields, Lilli climbs into her sleeping loft, moody and despairing, to reread the letters from Mutti that she has been receiving regularly since the first one arrived back in January. In February, Mutti wrote that, *"I am working in a beauty salon here in Amsterdam, washing the clients' hair and other small duties. The owner is a member of the Dutch resistance and she is kind to us, letting us use the rooms in the back of the shop. Your sisters are learning to speak Dutch."*

Lilli is pleased that her family is safe for the time being. But she knows all too well how precarious their situation is.

A month later, Mutti writes: *"I cannot understand why you have not yet received an answer from your uncle. You must write to him again. Ships sailing between England and America are being torpedoed in the Atlantic by German submarines. Their cargoes have been sunken or confiscated. So, try again. It is very important that you contact him."*

Lilli, of course, had already written him twice. She is anxiously awaiting a reply from America when Mutti's most recent letter arrives. It chills Lilli to the bone. *"I am sending you a parcel, Lilli, of some things I have with me here that I do not need. Some small pieces of jewelry, not very valuable but pretty, a few items of lingerie, and my flowered chiffon dress. I know these things are not suitable on the farm, but perhaps you will wear them in America."*

This letter sends a message that is disturbingly clear: The Nazi takeover of the Netherlands is imminent, and Lilli's mother and sisters will be in danger of being sent off to one of the internment camps for Jews. Mutti's letters will then stop, and contact between Lilli and her family will be severed.

Lilli is lying face down on her bed in a puddle of tears, when voices from the kitchen below drift up to her.

"I've made up my mind, Wilf. She's got to go."

"Ah no, Aggie, no need to be so harsh toward the girl. Not her fault about Tim getting hurt."

"It's not only that. She's useless in the garden. Works like she's some kind of a fairy princess. Comes from some rich Jewish family back there in Germany, I'm sure. *And* she's getting too old."

"*Old!* How old? Twelve?"

"More like thirteen. I've seen you looking at her, Wilf, with sore eyes. I know what's going on around here."

Lilli leaps out of her bed. Although she's heard every word the Rathbones have said, she still can't believe her ears. They are sending her away! In many ways, she won't be sorry to leave, as her eight months here have been sad and difficult. While she adores Tim and has enjoyed caring for him and returning his affection, her hopes for school and learning English amounted to nothing. As to life on the farm, the Rathbones have never asked her any questions about her former life, or her family. Lilli has also noticed their stinginess with the food they serve her. She's never said anything when they've given fresh white bread and sweet biscuits to Tim, but set out a stale loaf and broken biscuits—bought cheaply from the baker's truck—for her, or when Mrs. Rathbone gave fried bacon to Tim, but only offered Lilli the drippings. Staying clean on the farm, with only cold water available, has made bathing and attending to her personal needs difficult. Lilli always feels dirty and is nauseated by the smells of chickens and manure. And she hates digging up the soil for the vegetable planting, with Mr. Rathbone leaning his sweaty body so close to hers.

But, despite all that, she wonders where will she go when she leaves the Rathbones?

Early in May, a massive bombing war, the German *blitzkrieg*, erupts over Holland. Within days, the nation surrenders to Hitler, and its Jewish population, as well as its refugees from other parts of Nazi-dominated Europe, are ordered to register. Jews must give up their radios. They may not own arms of any kind. They must sew the yellow star onto their garments, with the word *Jood*, Dutch for Jew, spelled out in the center.

Dutch citizens, like the woman who has been sheltering Mutti and the girls, are now themselves in danger. Can Mutti and Lilli's sisters go deep enough underground to remain hidden, or will they be caught and sent to one of the concentration camps in Germany or Poland? Even if they can remain hidden, what will the family eat? How will they live? Will Mutti ever be able to write another letter to Lilli? Even if she does, will Lilli ever receive it?

At the same time, Lilli has been told by Mrs. Rathbone that arrangements have been made for her to live on a farm hostel, some distance away in the next county.

One morning, so early that the first roosters have just begun to crow, Mrs. Rathbone appears at the top of the ladder that leads to the sleeping loft. "Today's the day," she informs Lilli. "Get up and pack your things, my girl. Mr. Rathbone will be driving you to the hostel. It's a long way, so best get an early start."

Seven

Once again, Lilli finds herself bouncing through the English countryside in the broken-down Rathbone farm truck. Her eyes are brimming with tears that she tries to hide from Mr. Rathbone by turning her head toward the passenger side window.

"Now, now, what's all this about?" he asks in a growly but not unsympathetic voice as he reaches across and pats her knee. "I can't reckon you're all that sorry to leave the farm."

Lilli nudges her body closer to the door of the truck. "No," she answers uncomfortably. "It's her. I can't believe she wouldn't let me say goodbye to Tim.

"How could she be so cruel to him? It's not for me I'm crying."

"Ah, that's a good girl then. But you know what Aggie is like. She didn't want him gettin' upset."

"But he will be upset when he wakes up and finds I'm gone. He was my only friend, and I was his. He'll hate me now forever. He won't understand."

Mr. Rathbone allows himself another pat of Lilli's

knee before returning his hand to the steering wheel. Lilli retreats into her own thoughts. She has no idea what this agricultural hostel will be like, though she can imagine more farm work with chickens, rabbits, goats, probably even pigs. Where will she eat and sleep? Who will her companions be? Even greater are her worries about her sisters and Mutti. Even if Mutti is able to write to her from Holland after the Nazi takeover, will she even get her letters? And what if mail eventually comes from her uncle in America? Mrs. Rathbone promised, with a nod of annoyance, that anything that arrived for Lilli would be forwarded to her at the hostel. But how can Lilli put her trust in a woman who would deceive her own child?

It is mid-morning now. Lilli must have dozed off after having been awakened at such an early hour. Mr. Rathbone has stopped the truck in front of a roadside pub. "Time for a bit of refreshment," he says, raising a curled hand to his lips. "Come down, m'girl, and we'll get you a lemonade and some crisps. Or maybe a sandwich."

In a half-awake daze, Lilli follows Mr. Rathbone as he crunches across the car park. In front of them sits a picturesque two-story whitewashed stone building with a slate roof. As they enter the building, Lilli inhales the stale, mixed scent of yeast and tobacco. But the room has a cozy, rustic air. Men standing at the bar drinking from large mugs eye Lilli and Mr. Rathbone indifferently for a moment, before returning to their pints.

"M'daughter," Mr. Rathbone says to the man behind the bar. "She'll just have a lemonade. And," he asks Lilli, "what'll you have to eat, dear?"

Lilli, who is starving, selects a cheese-and-pickle sandwich. Mr. Rathbone then walks her over to the "nook," a table wedged between the fireplace and a small, glazed window, at some distance from the bar. Once he sees that she's comfortably settled and has her food, Mr. Rathbone returns to the bar, where the men are lined up at their places like birds perched on a roof ledge.

Lilli eats her meal alone, while Mr. Rathbone stands at the bar, the voices of the men growing louder and more boisterous. Mr. Rathbone has apparently made friends with his drinking companions, and orders a round of beers for everybody.

Nearly an hour goes by before they return to the truck. Mr. Rathbone is red-faced, and his gait is unsteady. "Ah, for a nice nap in a lay-by, now," he remarks in a deep, blowsy voice as he starts the engine. "Wouldn't you like that, m'dear?"

Lilli isn't sure what a lay-by is, and she doesn't want to find out. "Mrs. Rathbone said they'd be expecting us at the hostel by mid-afternoon," she retorts. Although she does not know what lies ahead for her, she cannot wait to rid herself of this man. She has never felt such a strong sense of danger before, not even in the presence of the dreaded Captain Koeppler.

With immense relief, Lilli jumps down from the farm truck, which has come to a stop in front of a long, low, barracks-like building. Mr. Rathbone has already descended and collected Lilli's meager possessions. He stands before her, smiling. "Well, I got ya here now, didn't I?" He moves closer to her. "Now give us a kiss for old times' sake, darlin', and I'll be off."

In a flash, Lilli reaches down, snatches her suitcase and backpack, and dashes toward what appears to be the main entrance to the building. A tall woman with popping blue eyes and whitish-blonde hair is standing on the threshold.

"Gracious, child, have you come directly from your billet?"

Lilli knows that the word *billet* refers to her host family. She nods breathlessly.

"I'm Mrs. Mayhew," the women announces, "the warden here at the hostel. Come through. I want to have a look at you. I assume you've brought your documents?"

Lilli digs into her backpack and produces her Kindertransport visa and her original passport.

"Hmm. Helga Frankfurter. You're only twelve, much

too young for us here. Although you're tall, and you do look somewhat mature for your years."

Lilli's insides shrink with worry. Suppose Mrs. Mayhew refuses her accommodation and she has to go to another billet like the Rathbones? Or someplace even worse.

They enter what looks like a sort of lobby, with two large desks and various billboards displaying names and work schedules, and some photos of the young women who presumably live and work here. Mrs. Mayhew sits down at one of the desks and gestures for Lilli to take a seat across from her. She is shaking her head. "Dear oh dear, your garments will have to be burned, all of them. And your hair, child. We'll want to undo those braids and cut it short."

Lilli's hand flies to her head. She hasn't washed her hair in a long time because Mrs. Rathbone refused to let her use the fuel to heat the water. Most of her clothes are the ones she brought from Germany, along with a few outsize army-issue garments she acquired while at the Rathbones.

"How often were you able to wash your clothing or bathe at your billet?" Mrs. Mayhew inquires kindly.

Something in the tenderness of the warden's voice brings Lilli to tears.

"Never mind," Mrs. Mayhew says quickly. "We'll have you in a warm tub in no time, and issue you a new wardrobe. But what sort of assignment we can give you here, I have no idea. Our young women must be seventeen to work on the farm or with the animals. So your stay," she finishes, "may be only temporary."

It's evening now, and following a supper of baked beans, sliced ham, and hot cocoa, Lilli is sitting on her dormitory bed, admiring her new clothing. In keeping with what Mrs. Mayhew called the "land girls'" uniform, she's received two short-sleeved shirts, a pullover, a warm jacket, breeches that can be tucked into the high rubber boots she was given, socks and shoes, and even a hat and a raincoat. Although the colors of the outer garments are a dreary greenish-gray, the wardrobe is sumptuous. Lilli has also had her promised bath, in a porcelain tub, with plenty of soap and hot water. Before that, a large-bosomed woman named Miss Plum, who is in charge of the dormitories, cut Lilli's hair and washed it in one of the bathroom sinks.

Lilli has also been introduced to the other girls in her dormitory. Most come from small English towns, and have uprooted themselves to work the land in place of the men who have gone off to war. The girls are a cheerful and giggly lot who tease each other gently, and look to engage in harmless pranks. They are, of course, very curious about Lilli. "Oh, I do hope they let you stay," says freckle-faced Maude, who has just finished telling Lilli about being kicked by a cow while milking this morning. "You would be like a younger sister."

A large and very tall young woman named Alice, who has quite a different British accent from Maude's, remarks, "Oh, I doubt our Helga would be up to hay-making, or bathing sheep. In any case, it would all be very irregular."

Lilli sighs. "I worked hard at the Rathbones, scrubbing floors, cleaning out the hen houses, digging the soil for planting ..."

"Not to worry, love," Maude adds hastily. "They've given you the uniform, so they're not likely to send you off so quickly."

Even though her new bed has a real mattress, clean sheets, and a soft pillow, Lilli's first night at the hostel is filled with troubling images and memories. She sees the leering eyes of Mr. Rathbone as he attempted to kiss her goodbye. The sound of the other girls' voices make her realize how desperately lonely she's been for human companionship. And Maude's mention of Lilli being a "younger sister" makes her think of her family hiding out in Nazi-dominated Holland or, worse, being transported to one of the camps.

Breakfast very early the next morning consists of hot porridge and milky tea. The rest of the hostelers then go off to work, while the cook comes out of the kitchen to meet the new arrival. Mrs. Mayhew is present. "Turn about, girl, and let me have a look at you," says the cook, a short round woman with a rosy complexion and carrot-orange hair. "Have you had any kitchen experience? I need a girl to help out and . . ." she surveys Lilli's height, "to reach up into the tall cupboards."

"Always at home, I helped my mother in the kitchen," Lilli replies eagerly.

"Hmm," says the cook, whose name is Mrs. Trumbull, "that doesn't mean much. But you're young and you'll learn." She turns to Mrs. Mayhew. "Well, it's all up to you."

A short time later, Lilli finds herself in the hostel's kitchen, wearing a cap and overalls, learning where the foods and utensils are stored, and being taught how to cook on a coal-fired stove.

A few weeks after Lilli's arrival at the hostel, a parcel from Mutti arrives. It was mailed just before the Dutch surrender to the Nazis, and was forwarded, after all, by Mrs. Rathbone.

Lilli's dormitory mates make cooing sounds of admiration as she tearfully opens the parcel and delicately removes the carefully wrapped items. Mutti's pearls have been secreted in the package, as have several rings and a brooch set with semi-precious stones. There are also sheer, delicately embroidered undergarments, and the wonderful flowered chiffon dress that Mutti wore the day she took Lilli to the Kindertransport.

Maude clasps Lilli, who is heaving with sobs. "Don't cry, love. You'll see your family again. Your mother just wants you to have some nice things to cheer you up a bit."

Lilli shakes her head vehemently. She knows that isn't why Mutti sent the parcel. She and the girls are going to the camps to die, while Lilli is safe.

Alice, with her disdainful manner and upper-class accent, replaces her glasses and kneels down beside Lilli's cot. "Tell you what," she says in a mothering tone. "You will come to the dance with us on Saturday. You'll take off your grubby old work clothes, fluff out your hair, put on a dab of lipstick, and wear this beautiful dress."

"Yes, yes!" the others exclaim. "Helga must come to the dance."

"We have a wonderful band," adds shy, pale-faced Elsie. "They play all the modern hits. Of course, we have no men to dance with, so we dance with each other. And there are refreshments."

Lilli shakes her head "no." It is impossible to think of such frivolity at this time, or ever.

Nonetheless, on Saturday evening, Lilli finds herself sharing the anticipatory fever of her dormitory mates. The young women are rummaging through their belongings for party clothes, and primping before the mirror. (Some of the girls slept the previous night in hair curlers derived from rags and hairpins.) They discard their high rubber boots and sturdy oxfords for uncomfortable high-heeled shoes in which they stagger about delightedly. Maude lends Lilli an extra pair, and offers her eyebrow pencil, rouge, and lipstick.

Lilli says she can't see why the girls are getting so fancied up. "It'll only be us there."

"Oh, no," says Maude. "There are some farmers from roundabout who come. Of course, they are older men. But then there's the band. You'll see."

When everyone is finally ready, they all get on bicycles and peddle off to the village hall. The hall is brightly lit, and decorated with banners celebrating the British war effort: DIG FOR VICTORY! ENLIST! ALWAYS CARRY YOUR GAS MASK!

A refreshment table is laid out with pitchers of punch, sweet biscuits and buns, and bowls of crisps. The most festive feature is the music. A band of surprisingly young men—perhaps they are unfit for fighting, Lilli wonders?—are playing a peppy American hit song, *Beer Barrel Polka*. Older British couples, as well as younger women in pairs, are stomping around the floor vigorously, feet flying, to the insistent rhythm.

Lilli has never heard this music before, and she is mesmerized.

The band follows with a slow number, *The White Cliffs of Dover*, a British favorite that is also popular in the United States. Lilli dances with Alice to the dream-like, yearning melody, and finds, to her surprise, that she is enjoying herself.

Other slow numbers follow—*April Showers* and *I'll Be Seeing You*—with Elsie telling Lilli the lyrics to the latter song, about lovers parted by war. "These words are beautiful and so sad," Lilli says. She asks Elsie if she has a boyfriend. Elsie replies that she does. He is fighting with the British forces trying to repel the Nazis in Scandinavia.

Finally, the band strikes up a lively number, also from America, called *Don't Sit Under the Apple Tree*. This time Lilli dances with sprightly, blonde Muriel, who attends to the larger farm animals back at the hostel. Muriel teaches Lilli the fast rhythm and swinging steps of the tune, and they wind down their escapade standing directly in front of the bandstand. Lilli finds herself facing the young man at the piano, whose eyes are so sharply fixed on her that her cheeks become fiery. She averts his gaze, letting her attention roam to the faces of the other musicians. They are all young, many still in their late teens. When she allow herself a second glance at the pianist, he smiles and waves to her in a friendly way, as if they know each other. Baffled, she turns to Muriel, who is beaming with delight and, along with the rest of the girls, reaching up to shake hands with the musicians, who are taking a break.

"It is strange," Lilli says to Muriel. "They are not in the Army?"

Muriel gives Lilli a questioning look. "No. Can't you tell? These fellows aren't Brits. They're prisoners of war . . . Germans. Most of them were shot down in flights over England."

Lilli is aghast. "Nazis!"

Muriel nods.

"Why aren't they in prison?"

"They are," says Muriel. "Haven't you seen the Nissen huts down the road from the hostel?"

Lilli is irate. "They are the enemy! How can you let them mix with you?"

"They aren't the leaders," Muriel tries to explain. "They're only boys who were forced into fighting by Nazi propaganda. Listen, Lilli, you have got to be . . ."

Lilli won't listen. "I am a Jew," she shrills. "These people killed my Papa." She runs from the hall, retrieves her bicycle, and rides her way by flashlight in the direction of the hostel.

Eight

The English summer has arrived, but Lilli finds the weather surprisingly cool and rainy, especially when compared with her last summer in Germany, when she and Helga spent time outdoors in the hot, dank garden at the Bayers.

The farm is thriving, and the hostelers are busy gathering up root vegetables and the early plantings of cabbage, carrots, and lettuce. Because of complaints about the dullness of the food served to the farm workers—mashed turnips, beets in vinegar, and boiled cabbage—Mrs. Trumbull has taught Lilli how to make special treats like rabbit stew, as well as sweet desserts and puddings.

Today, Lilli is strolling along one of the country lanes in search of wild berries for her fruit cobbler. She comes upon a clump of blackberry bushes that lure her off the road and into a gently shaded area, where the fruit is ripe and abundant. As Lilli wanders contentedly from shrub to shrub, tasting the juicy, sweet berries, she experiences a moment of contentment with her present life. Even though the letters from Mutti have stopped coming since the Nazi invasion of Holland, she finally received a letter from Papa's brother in America. Uncle Herman told her he cannot promise much, as it is impossible to bring Jewish refugees into the United States at this time. The quotas are extremely limited and, while the US government supports Britain in its struggle to hold off Nazi Germany, most American citizens oppose entering the war. Perhaps, if America did become involved, he writes, things might change. Lilli is disappointed, of course, but she never expected that getting to America was going to be a simple matter.

When Lilli emerges from the undergrowth, with her well-filled tin bucket, she finds herself on an unfamiliar stretch of the dirt road. From where she is standing, she can clearly see the odd-looking Nissen huts in which the POW's are quartered. The huts look like huge semi-circular logs, and are newly made of corrugated iron that gleams in the sun.

Suddenly, Lilli sees the figure of a man in the near distance. He is wearing a brightly colored yellow vest over his drab prison uniform, and there is a large letter *P* painted on his trouser leg. He is bent over, clipping the weedy roadside verge. One of the Nazi prisoners! Lilli cringes in panic and turns quickly to hide herself in the foliage. She's barely out of sight when she hears a voice calling softly in German, "Fraulein, don't worry. I think you know me."

The sound of her home country's language is both familiar and frightening to Lilli. She writes her letters to Mutti in German, of course, but she hasn't heard German words spoken out loud since the last Nazi official left the Kindertransport as the train crossed the border into Holland.

The young man is right. Lilli does know him. He is the POW who played the piano at the dance, whose eyes had remained fixed on her for an embarrassingly long time. Even then, he had waved at her as if they knew each other.

He comes toward her through the underbrush and his friendly smile is the same as it was on the evening that Lilli fled the dance hall. "You are always running from me," he says. "I am sorry if I frightened you. My name is Karl Becker. Yes, I am a prisoner of war. Our plane was shot down just off the British coast a month ago."

Lilli is speechless. Her eye is drawn to a long smooth scar on the prisoner's left cheek, as from a severe burn. She also noticed that he stumbled toward her with a slight limp. However, she knows he won't harm her. Carol and the other hostelers had calmed her after her flight from the dance by explaining the British policy of treating POWs humanely unless they are suspected of being strong Nazi supporters or having knowledge of German military plans. Most POWs are not even required to work, but many do to keep busy; on the roads, digging ditches, rebuilding bombed-out homes, even on the farms at harvesting time.

"Have you been wounded?" Lilli finally asks. She finds it hard to take her eyes off his shiny scar.

"Not so badly as the others," he replies. "Our *Luftwaffe* Captain was killed with another officer of our crew of four. The other survivor is missing a limb. He was sent to a British military hospital. So, you see, I've been lucky." He finds a grassy patch of ground and sits down, gesturing for Lilli to do the same. After a moment of hesitation, she joins him. She offers him some of the blackberries she picked. He takes only a few, saying, "You will not have enough for your baking."

Karl then tells Lilli a little about his past. He was a ten-year-old music student when he was first recruited into the Hitler Youth. When he entered his teens, his father, who had been an airman in the First World War, insisted that Karl apply for the *Flieger*, the flying division. "I cared nothing for either fighting or flying; only the piano. But the father is supreme in the German household. So this is what happened." Karl seems to harbor deep resentment toward his father, as well as his mother, who deserted the family when Karl was forced to enter the *Flieger*. He tells Lilli sadly, "I don't think I will ever go back to Germany."

Lilli is magnetized by Karl's story. She sees that he, too, has been a victim, as were many boys growing up under Hitler. Too innocent to understand the real meaning of the Nazi creed, they were drawn into the militaristic youth movement, attracted by the uniform, the banners, the bugles, and the drums. They were taught to sing the Hitler Youth "Jewish blood" marching song: *And when Jewish blood spurts from the knife, then things will again go well.* They were pressured by their friends and, in Karl's case, by a father who had dreams of a son in the *Luftwaffe.*

Lilli wants to hear more, but she has to get back to the kitchen to start the evening meal. She gets up and bids Karl goodbye. He smiles at her, then rises from the ground and walks toward the Nissen huts.

Mrs. Trumbull looks somewhat cross when Lilli comes flying into the kitchen a few minutes late. However, she softens at the sight of the bucket full of plump blackberries. Lilli quickly wraps herself in an apron and begins to prepare the pastry dough in a whirl of flour.

"Where did you get these lovelies, dear?" Mrs. Trumbull asks as she begins peeling the vegetables.

Lilli gulps. "Oh, quite far down the road. I could even see the Nissen huts from there."

Mrs. Trumbull interrupts her vegetable peeling, and waves the sharp knife in Lilli's direction. "Don't go down there again, my girl. You don't want to meet one of them POWS working on the roads."

Lilli shudders. How could Mrs. Trumbull know what happened? Still she asks, "Why? Are they dangerous? They play in the band at the dance hall on Saturday nights. The girls are quite friendly with them. They tell me they're harmless young Germans who were dragged into the Nazi ranks by Hitler's propaganda."

"Harmless, are they? We Brits are too soft on them. Think if it was the other way around, if they got their hands on an English prisoner?"

Lilli has to agree that the Nazis would probably be as barbarously cruel to their war prisoners as they have been to the Jews. But shouldn't some nation set an example of trying to deal justly, even with an enemy, she wonders?

"Don't go fraternizin' with them fellows," says Mrs. Trumbull with a big chop of her knife. "Those be my last words on the subject."

It is Saturday, and the girls are pleased to learn that Lilli, despite what happened last time, is going to the dance hall with them. "So you've gotten over it," Muriel says with relief. "We girls must have a bit of fun now and then, you know, or we'll all become as dull as turnips."

Lilli wears her flowered chiffon dress again. It makes her think of her mother, and a wave of sadness envelops her. Still, this is the dress that Mutti hoped Lilli might one day wear in America. Even if Lilli never gets there, she has friends, plenty of food and a clean bed. And she has met Karl. England, it turns out, is not so bad. America can wait.

The dance hall is even more aglow to Lilli this evening, and it is impossible for her not to gaze toward the raised platform where the band is already playing. Karl is there, having seen her immediately, and he smiles and lifts one hand from the keyboard in his characteristic wave.

Lilli is soon dancing, with Alice, with Muriel, with Maude. Then an older man, one of the local farmers, asks her to dance. His grip is clumsy and he isn't as nimble as her female partners. But Lilli, who hasn't danced with any man except Papa when she was a little girl, experiences the pleasure of having matured beyond her childish years.

Lilli's dance with her male partner ends, and the musicians go off on their break. Alice comes rushing up to her with a concerned frown. "Lilli, you are beet-red. Come and sit down."

Lilli takes her leave politely and lets Alice lead her to a quiet corner behind the refreshment table. Alice draws out a handkerchief and wipes Lilli's brow in her typical motherly fashion. "Are you well? I've never seen you this way."

"I'm fine," Lilli protests. "I'm having such a good time."

"Sit here, and I'll get you something cool to drink," Alice commands. But Lilli is already on her feet. "Don't trouble. I'll get it myself." Lilli is surprised that she is brazen enough to walk away from Alice, but her eye has noticed Karl leaving the dance hall, cigarette already lit.

However, when she peers out the door, wanting to say a few words to him, she loses her courage. Mrs. Trumbull would surely call this "fraternizin'," she thinks to herself. Lilli isn't even sure why she is so drawn to this slight young man, with his scar and his limp. He feels as familiar to her as an older brother, or a fellow orphan, stripped of family, with a blank future.

It is now the autumn of 1941. More than a year has slipped by. The *Luftwaffe* has stepped up its Blitz in order to weaken Britain in preparation for a land invasion. The countryside is no longer spared, as German bombers seek to destroy the British aircraft industry and the airfields of the Royal Air Force.

Although the hostel is not very far from one of Britain's hidden strategic air commands, there have luckily been no direct hits so far. Every day, Mrs. Mayhew keeps a worried eye on the sky.

The land-army girls continue with their neverending farm tasks: milking, shoveling manure, digging and planting, hoeing and harvesting. And the threshing season is here again. The first time Lilli witnessed the arrival of the enormous, throbbing, horse-drawn machine, steam-powered and fitted with crushers and spikes, she was shocked to learn that some of her fellow hostelers had actually volunteered to work at threshing. Feeding the machine, which separates the wheat grains from the chaff, means climbing the narrow, shaking ladder to the top, cutting the binder off the sheath, and inserting the sheaves into the maw of the noisy monster.

"I'd not do it for all the pearls in India," Maude declared.

"Nor I," added Elsie. "Not even if they paid us more than the extra bit they do."

But Alice was thrilled to do what she called, "a real man's job."

"Don't see how you can do it," Maude retorted. "It's not only the fearful noise and the choking dust. It's all the mice and huge rats, escaping and scurrying around in the grain fields."

The great machine arrives at the hostel's wheat field. This year, a POW crew has been assigned to help with the job. Karl, of course, is among them. Counter to Mrs. Trumbull's accusations of "fraternizin'," the girls and the young men, many of whom already know each other from the dance hall or from other cooperative farm work, are as casual as old friends.

For Lilli, Karl has become a warm companion, the only person in all of England who knows that her name isn't Helga, and that she is fourteen years old. He also knows about Kristallnacht, when they took Papa away forever. He knows about her hiding out with the Bayers and about Mutti and the mysterious Captain Koeppler. And Karl even knows how it came about that Lilli substituted for Helga at the last minute.

"I will never forgive myself for what happened, unless and until I find Helga," Lilli told him one day. "This guilt I must live with all my life."

"Your intentions were for the best," he answered. "If Helga is alive, I promise you will find her after the war."

Lilli's eyes flooded with tears.

Curiosity and the delivery of lunch for the hostelers has drawn Lilli into the fields to observe the threshing. From a distance, it looks like a great party of happy harvest workers, merrily tossing the sheaves about and shouting to one another. But on closer inspection, it's more like a deafening dust storm from hell. The air is thick with the dried debris forked up from the haystacks and buzzing and whirring insects, disturbed by all the activity. And, true to Maude's description, panicked field mice are definitely underfoot. Fortunately, the land girls are well-protected, having covered their heads and tucked their pants legs into heavy socks.

It's a great relief when the wildly pulsating machine is finally turned off and the threshers break for lunch. Lilli distributes the sandwiches and tea, and sits with the other girls in a wagon drawn up beside the horses that pull the thresher, who are now quietly grazing on ample amounts of spilled grain. The POWS have all come down off the stilled machine, except for Karl. He has climbed to the very top and appears to be making some sort of repair. He looks so alone up there, his stark figure silhouetted against the sky.

Suddenly, one of the horses harnessed to the thresher violently kicks up a rear leg and emits a skittish sound, almost like a human shriek. The horse then takes off, tilting its heavy burden sharply to the right.

Lilli jumps down to the ground and screams out in German, "Karl, Karl! Take care! Jump clear, before it's too late!" The machine with its great metal teeth and formidable weight is beginning to topple.

Lilli's call of alarm has alerted the other POWs. But they can do little except run fearfully alongside the moving menace. Karl is now clinging to a precarious foothold on the swinging ladder that he has kicked loose, for the purpose of making the broadest jump possible. Lilli cannot bear to look. Will he be able to leap before the thresher crashes to the ground on top of him?

The thresher drivers have now subdued and halted the runaway horse. But it is too late to right the badly off-balance thresher. It overturns with a hideous thud and an enormous clanging. At the same time a great cheer goes up. Lilli opens her eyes. Karl is safe. She rushes away to the privacy of the hostel kitchen, shaking with terror and weeping with relief.

* * *

Several months later, in December 1941, a world-shaking event that will alter the outcome of World War II takes place, and the United States enters the battle to defeat Hitler. All of England is jubilant. Uncle Herman writes that in the new year, he hopes to be able to bring Lilli to America.

The future, however, still appears dreamy and vague to Lilli. It is only when her uncle writes that papers are being drawn up and that she will sail by merchant ship from Liverpool in the summer of 1942 that she begins to panic. The sea voyage will be dangerous, as German submarines prowl the waters of the Atlantic. But Lilli is more distraught at the thought of leaving her good friends at the hostel. And she will never see Karl again. They have become as close as sister and brother as they have shared the confidences of the lost.

On the day Lilli leaves, there are teary goodbyes. "Give our love to America!" the hostelers shout as she is driven off in an Army lorry, with her land army uniform and a few personal belongings. "Give me your address in America," yells Karl. "I promise to write. If you will."

PART II

1942-1946

Nine

My name is Lilli Frankfurter. I am nineteen years old, and a sophomore at one of the well-regarded women's colleges, known as the Seven Sisters, in the northeastern United States. It is 1946 and World War II has ended, leaving behind a trail of horror stories, death, and human debris. I want desperately to go back to Europe to search for my lost family, so I've been taking journalism courses. I'm thinking that maybe one day I can get a job as a foreign correspondent!

Dr. Barbara Bagby, my journalism professor, tells me bluntly that I'm "aiming high, especially for a woman." I don't think she's a very good spokesperson for a women's college. She maintains a neutered, austere appearance: tight lips, wire-rimmed eyeglasses, and straight lemony-yellow hair in an unflattering Dutch-boy cut. In her unemotional, nasal voice, she reminds me that I'm not Ernest Hemingway or any of the other great writers and foreign correspondents who are now swarming all over the ravaged continent and filing reports in American magazines and newspapers. Still, my unenthusiastic mentor makes a suggestion: "Write me something, let's say in the form of a memoir or a journal. Let's see if you can bring a recent experience to life. Why don't you tell me what it was really like to come to America, after growing up in Nazi Germany and wartime England?"

At first, I'm not sure I want to write about the years since 1942, when I arrived in America during the thick of the war. Back then, I was homesick for a past that was a mixture of deep family love and unbearable loss. I also wasn't very nice to my American relatives and hosts, who were to give me everything I now have. It wasn't their fault that they looked upon me like a visitor from another planet. Because of my mysterious past in a savage world, I wasn't an ordinary person; I was a specimen. The Americans didn't know how to learn about me, so they probed me from all angles, like a meteorite that had fallen to earth, and asked questions that aroused too many bad memories.

I'm going to start by writing this in rough form to work out all the tangles that may be too personal for a finished piece. I'll begin with my arrival and then the shock of meeting that awful child, that noisy chatterbox with the hoarse demanding voice whose name was Isabel.

I spent most of the ghastly sea voyage in my bunk on that creaking and clanking merchant ship, seasick and tearful. We docked somewhere in New Jersey. I never saw the famed Statue of Liberty or the New York City skyline.

The Frankfurters, Uncle Herman and Aunt Harriette, met me full of apologies and worries, and could not have been more solicitous. I had hoped that my uncle, being Papa's older brother, would somehow resemble him and bring flickering images of him back to me. But this was not the case. My uncle was full-faced and balding, pleasant, but on the quiet side. His mind seemed to be somewhere else, taken up perhaps with his business and finance operations. He had emigrated from Germany in his university years and seemed, as I would later observe, a typical American male. He had only the slightest remaining trace of a foreign accent.

Aunt Harriette, on the other hand, was something else entirely. She was lively and outgoing, in personality and appearance: a short, full-breasted woman with narrow hips and elegant legs, dressed in a white-linen summer suit with a colorful scarf. Her hair was a rich, carroty red that matched her lipstick and her nail polish. Her eyes were ringed with liner, black kohl. Glittering gold jewelry adorned her bosom, her ears, and her wrists. I couldn't help liking her, with her rapid speech and rapid enthusiasms. "We'll shop and get you an entire new wardrobe," she said after we had arrived at the enormous wood-and-stone house in Westchester, an upscale New York City suburb. We were sorting through my pathetic land army belongings. "I can't believe you even brought your rubber Wellington boots!" she exclaimed. We had all worn Wellies on the farm, as there was mud every-where. (I had long ago regretfully given up the beautiful fallen-apart leather boots that Grossmutter Bayer had bought me at the Kaufhaus.)

"Mind if we toss these?" Aunt Harriette asked with a twinkle. "I know where I can get you a pair of really magnificent leather hiking boots."

We were sitting in the upstairs bedroom that Aunt Harriette had redecorated for me in white wicker, flow-ered chintz, and crisp organdy. The room resembled the very garden that it looked down upon, which was a riot of colorful blooms and neatly trimmed shrubs. It would have been impossible to visualize such a room in Germany, even in the most prosperous of homes, where the fashion for bedrooms was dark furniture and sedate wallpaper. The whiteness and the frilliness made me think of *schlag*—whipped cream—too much of which could be a digestive embarrassment.

Speaking of digestion, dinner at my aunt and uncle's home was in the "small" dining room, and was served by a friendly maid of long-standing whose name was Maggie. Even with the wartime rationing that had started to take place in America, there appeared to be no shortage of anything. For just the three of us (my aunt and uncle had no children), there was an abundant roast, tender and juicy, the likes of which I had never tasted. Dessert was homemade apple pie. I kept thinking of my hostel friends, eating baked beans on toast, to say nothing of the starving refugees and emaciated concentration camp victims all over Europe. Why couldn't Helga and Elspeth and Mutti have been given the chance to emigrate too? Why hadn't Papa pressed earlier and harder for his brother to help us come to America? Perhaps he'd been too proud; maybe he hadn't seen clearly enough what was coming with the rise of Hitler.

Despite their kindness, it amazed me how little my aunt and uncle asked me about my life in Germany and England. They seemed to be satisfied with my description of the farm hostel as "a cross between an army camp and a boarding school," and they accepted my loose description of the Rathbones' poultry farm without further inquiry. Perhaps they just didn't know what questions to ask. More than likely, they simply couldn't have imagined the sleeping loft that I shared with small scurrying creatures, or the frozen chamber pots and vile outhouse, draped with spider webs.

In any case, I volunteered no information beyond the basics. Was I ashamed or embarrassed by my experiences? I think neither. I was simply angry, angry that Papa had surely died and that the others, if not hidden away, were almost certainly doomed to share his fate.

"We have got to get you out into the country air," Aunt Harriette kept insisting during my first weeks in

Westchester, which seemed country-like enough to me, with its broad greenery and woodsy areas for pleasant strolls. "Besides," she explained, "you need to have a friend. She's a little younger than you are, but bright as a penny. I think you two are going to get along famously." A week or so later, I found myself being driven in the back seat of Uncle Herman's shiny, new Cadillac to what Aunt Harriette referred to as a "modest summer hotel in the Catskills."

She sounded almost apologetic as she explained from the front seat that Shady Pines was a simple, family-run place. It was there that I would meet my new friend, Isabel Brandt, who was vacationing with her parents. "Sally—Isabel's mother—and I have been dear friends since our early school days, long before I met your uncle. We are truly like sisters." The word *sisters* was always upsetting to me, especially now, when I was convinced I was living the life that Helga should have had. I had, of course, always written to my uncle as Helga, and my new family did not know of my false identity.

"Remember, Helga dear," said my aunt a few hours later, as we crunched off the paved road onto one of dirt and stones, with deep wheel ruts and a hump in the center, "this place is really rustic. The accommodations are . . . well, a bit crude. You'll be sharing a room with Isabel, and the toilet and shower facilities are outside. I hope that will be all right."

Aunt Harriette escorted me to the room I was to share with Isabel. "She's twelve," my aunt advised me, "and still has a bit of baby fat, but she's really very grown up. You'll find she's a typical American girl."

I had no way, of course, of knowing what that might be.

Aunt Harriette apologized again for the room's unpainted wood-plank walls and the shared bureau and closet, and left me to unpack. One of the two beds was undoubtedly Isabel's, as she had left her clothes and even her sneakers on top of the covers. So, I placed my things on the other one.

I was still bending over my suitcase when the "typical American girl" dashed into the room, unfastened the top of her bathing suit, gave me a horrified look, and announced, "You're in the wrong room. This one is mine."

When I told her, "I am Helga," she seemed to have no idea what I was talking about and, black eyes full of hostility, dashed off without explanation. So perhaps I was in the wrong room. I closed my suitcase, sat down on the bed, and waited.

Matters were soon sorted out. Apparently, no one had told Isabel that I was going to be her roommate, or anything at all about me. Aunt Harriette apologized, a bit vaguely, for Isabel's rudeness, saying her family had not expected me to arrive so early in the day, etc. We would all meet, and I'd be introduced at dinner that evening.

* * *

I'd been told that the meal would be served in the dining room of the hotel's main building, and that Shady Pines was known for its excellent kosher Jewish cuisine. As the clothes Aunt Harriette had bought me so far were on the casual side, I felt I should dress properly, so I put on Mutti's flowered-chiffon dress. It was, after all, the dress she had meant for me to wear in America.

The dining room was big and bright and noisy, with a hundred or more people seated at large round tables, tearing away at home-baked rolls, smearing them with chicken fat and chopped liver. The Friday night meal was going to contain meat, so no dairy products such as butter or milk would be served. I met Isabel's parents, both of whom seemed a little uncomfortable about the earlier mix-up. Her father wore dark-rimmed eyeglasses and had a small mustache. Her mother kept a vulture-like watch on Isabel, who was seated next to me. I had the feeling Isabel was being punished for having been so abrupt with me earlier, which wasn't completely her fault. Why had she been kept in the dark about my arrival?

Very soon, the food began to arrive. A suave waiter with a wrinkled, chalky-white face and black patent-leather hair swirled his tray of soups before me and set down a brimming bowl without spilling a drop. He called me a "beauty" and asked Isabel who I was. She told him I was "Helga from Germany," and whispered to me that he was Harry, the head waiter at the hotel for years, and nothing but an old flirt. Sure enough, when he'd finished serving the table, he blew me a kiss at me with two fingers.

Were all Americans so bold, I wondered? Another waiter, much younger—or maybe he was only a busboy—had been staring at me ever since I sat down.

My other embarrassing problem was the huge amount of food I was expected to eat. After a few table-spoons of the rich, golden-colored soup, I managed a chicken wing and some peas and carrots. For dessert there were baked apples and sponge cake and tea. By that time, word must have gotten around the dining room that there was a Jewish refugee girl from Germany at the Brandt-Frankfurter table. People who had already finished their meal came up to us, shaking their heads, and appraising me keenly. "Such a pretty girl," said one woman, who looked as though she ate well, "but too thin. You'll have to fatten her up, Sally." The woman was addressing Isabel's mother. But Aunt Harriette answered assertively that Americans ate too much. "Helga's been living on a wartime diet for a long time now. Our food is far too rich for her at present."

More Shady Pines' guests crowded around the table. There was such a hubbub, I could hardly make out what they were asking. One man, cigar in mouth, did catch my attention. "Did you ever see Hitler, that bum?" he called out in a booming voice. "Enough!" a woman, probably his wife, commanded. "Can't you see the poor child is exhausted? Let her be." Little by little, the inquirers and curiosity seekers drifted away. I was terribly confused. What did I want, questions or no questions? Why did I find these well-meaning Americans so disturbing? How was I ever going to adjust to life in the United States? At last, we all rose from the table. I looked to my left, where Isabel had been sitting. But she was gone. I had no idea when she'd made her escape.

The next morning, after a night of muddled and dreary dreams, I woke about two hours before breakfast and got ready to explore the countryside. This was something I had enjoyed so much while living at the hostel in England, after the restrictions of my years in Germany.

I was lacing up my hiking boots as quietly as possible when Isabel stirred and demanded sleepily to know where I was going. True, it was barely light out. When I told her I would be gone a couple of hours and asked if she'd like to accompany me, she groaned and dove under the covers.

I had learned all the old paths and trails in the English countryside around the hostel, and I had a pretty good eye for direction, so that I seldom got lost. There was something rougher and more challenging, however, in the tangling American "wilderness," even though it was not at all uninhabited, but dotted with small farms and homesteads, most of them in shabby condition, their yards filled with broken-down automobiles and rusted machinery. Unlike England, there seemed to be no fences, hedgerows, or other indications of boundaries. So it was hard to know whether or not I was trespassing. One moment I'd be making my way through dense forest, with heavy undergrowth, that seemed to be miles away from human habitation, while my next few steps would lead me to the front door of one of the neglected looking hovels.

I had just emerged from a dark copse of woods. There was no farmhouse or other dwelling in sight. But my ears were assaulted with the loud and vicious barking of a dog. I thought of backing into the forest and climbing a tree. But the animal found me out before I had the chance.

It was a huge, shaggy beast, not as sleek as the dogs in Germany that the SS and other police patrolled with, on leashes. Perhaps it was a good-natured animal, not that used to people but not trained, as in Germany, to tear at human flesh. This turned out not to be the case. The dog leapt at me in a frenzy, hurling its heavy body on top of mine. Teeth like sharpened steel spikes sank into my bare leg. I was on the ground, screaming, screaming, in pain and terror. But I could not hear the sounds I was making, only the hoarse, shrill barking of the attacking dog.

Ten

"Hey, hey . . . Hey."

I was slowly rising to the surface of some dark and fearsome place, yet the words in my ears were wondrously soft, and the barking of the hysterical hound had vanished. I opened my eyes to the whiteness of a sailor's middy and, above it, the fresh face of a young man with searching blue eyes.

The next moment the pain in my leg struck with such fierceness that I cried out.

"Yeah, you got a pretty deep gnashing there, girl." The voice now became a bit husky. "Take a deep breath, because I'm gonna lift you up and carry you. By the way, my name is Roy."

"Helga," I managed to breathe.

"Oh, a German name."

I wanted to answer, to explain that I was a Jewish refugee from Germany, but I must have passed out again. The next thing I heard was the revving of an automobile engine. Roy was strapping me into the passenger seat of a car. "I'm taking you into town to see the doctor. Can you hear me? Do you understand?"

"Yes, yes," I said. "You really mustn't trouble yourself." I looked down at the calf of my leg, which was now wrapped in white bandages stained with small rivulets of blood. "It was only a dog bite."

"Only," Roy mocked. "We've gotta get you a tetanus shot. Just cross your fingers that dog hasn't got rabies."

Rabies! My head began to whirl with visions of foaming at the mouth, hallucinations, paroxysms, brain disease, and *death*. "Do animals in America have rabies?"

"Sure. Bats, skunks, raccoons, foxes, wolves. A dog can get it from a wild- animal bite. But," Roy patted my knee, "there haven't been any reports of rabies around here for a while. So calm down. Where are you from, anyway?"

I told him briefly about Germany and then England.

"Oh, now I get it. Hey, I'm going to try a little home-grown German on you."

To my amazement and delight, Roy broke into my birth language, and I could make sense of his comforting words. It turned out that he was Irish on his father's side, but German on his mother's, and had been brought up partly by his grandmother.

More than an hour later, Roy drove me back to Shady Pines. The doctor in the nearby village of Harper's Falls had treated my wound with antiseptics, re-bandaged my leg, given me a tetanus shot, and assured me there had been no recent cases of rabies in the entire county. Still, I was given a list of symptoms to be aware of in the coming days, just to be safe.

Roy parked in the Shady Pines lot, and suggested that I lean on him as we approached the broad sweeping lawn that fronted the main building of the hotel. Already, I could hear a loud buzz of voices—I had been missing for hours. Once again, I had brought unwanted attention to myself, and had surely worried my relatives.

I made my appearance walking beside Roy, and limping as slightly as possible. But the sight of me drew a round of women's screams and, when Roy mentioned that I'd been bitten by a farm dog that we were sure *didn't* have rabies, Aunt Harriette promptly fainted.

In gratitude for rescuing me from "bleeding to death alone in the woods," Roy was invited to have lunch at Shady Pines, and the big fuss started all over again. The guests also wanted to know about Roy. He was seventeen, just out of boot camp, and awaiting assignment to a ship, probably somewhere in the Pacific. He had heard the barking dog and my screams from across the road, where there was a leafy, well-concealed bungalow colony where he had been visiting relatives for a few days.

Again, I was bombarded with questions from all over the dining room, this time as to whether I had any symptoms of rabies yet. "Does it burn where you were bitten?" "Have you got a headache?" "Can you drink water? Because you know that's why they call it hydrophobia.

If you can't, well . . ." It was a relief when I was ordered to spend the afternoon in my room, resting. "Show me where you'll be," Roy whispered before leaving. "I'll come by later and check on you, pretty girl." He spoke in German, and every time he did that, I felt a throb of familiarity. I thought of Karl, although he would not have been so personal.

Isabel, who I thought had been acting strangely all through lunch, was strictly warned by her mother to stay out of our room for a couple of hours so as not to disturb me. There also appeared to be something going on between her and Roy. When I glanced back after reaching our room, I saw her looking up at him and waving her arms around as if she knew him and was angry about something. Perhaps she was jealous of all the attention I'd been getting. I'd have been more than happy to transfer the whole glaring burden to her.

I had been resting for a while and had maybe even dozed off, when I opened my eyes and noticed that one of the bureau drawers that had been assigned to me wasn't properly closed. It sat open at an angle, as if an effort to slam it shut in a hurry had backfired.

Instantly suspicious, I rose from my bed, limped across the floorboards, and pulled the drawer open. Sure enough, someone had been examining my possessions while I'd been exploring the unfriendly countryside.

Most private was my *Shokoladen* box, which I had brought with me from Germany and treasured during my time at the Rathbones and at the hostel. It had never been tampered with before, to my knowledge. Now I could see that the mementos, photos, and letters had been sifted through. The picture with Mutti, Papa, and the three of us lay at a crooked angle. A letter, written in German, had been removed from its envelope and been reinserted the wrong way around. Isabel!

An inspection of the half of the closet where I had hung my things revealed more snooping. Hangers had been brushed aside for a closer look. My delicate flowered chiffon dress was crushed against another garment. I knew that Aunt Harriette, who was already familiar with my wardrobe and the contents of my old chocolate box, would have no need to invade my privacy. Isabel!

When would our stay at Shady Pines end and rid me of this "typical American girl?"

Was I dreaming, or was Roy really calling to me from the window above my bed? Darkness pervaded the room. I had no way of knowing if Isabel was asleep. But how long could I just lie there, with Roy urging me to come outside?

I had no time to think carefully about what I was doing. I got up and crouched close to the window. "One moment," I whispered hastily. I was wearing the flower-sprigged seersucker summer pajamas that Aunt Harriette had bought me—"with matching robe." Snatching up the latter, I tiptoed across the floor and let myself out the door. Roy met me at the bottom of the porch steps casually, as if there was nothing wrong with his invading Shady Pines in the middle of the night and enticing a fifteen-year-old girl to a rendezvous.

"How's your leg?" he asked. "Can you walk to the car? I parked just off the grounds. I could carry you."

"Car? No. Where are we going? It's crazy."

"Helga, listen. It's just so we can sit and talk. See, I got my orders yesterday. I have to be on the eight AM train to the city. I wanted to see you again. To say goodbye."

Limping only slightly, I followed Roy under a starlit sky to the borrowed car he had used to take me to the doctor that morning. He had parked it at the side of the dirt road, hidden by trees. He helped me into the passenger seat and came around to the driver's side. It felt odd to be sitting in a parked vehicle that wasn't about to go anywhere.

"So you must leave tomorrow," I said to break the silence that followed after he had gotten in the car. "I'm sad. I can only say thank you once again. Do you really think you will go to the Pacific?"

Roy flung his arm across the back of my seat. I could feel his fingers dangling loosely at the back of my neck. "Yeah," he mumbled. "But let's not talk about that now. I want to tell you some things in German. I hope you can understand me." I relaxed, looking forward to the kind of familiarity I had experienced in my sibling-like discussions with Karl. But what Roy told me in German made me blush and fidget, and long to get back to my room. His words were agonizingly personal, praising my hair, my eyes, my body. He spoke of feelings he had for me that he could barely suppress. His arm engaged my neck and he drew me to him in a smothering embrace. I pulled away sharply and opened the door of the car. "*Nein!* This is too much. You are asking me to pay a price for your services."

I ran, limping, back toward the grounds of the hotel, with Roy following me. "Listen to me, listen to me, Helga," he said after me. "I never meant to . . . I truly care for you. I acted like some American guy. I was stupid. I apologize." I slowed down. My bandaged leg had begun to hurt. "Wait," Roy begged. "Before we get too close to the hotel. Give me your address. I'll write to you. I swear I will. I don't want you to forget me. I won't forget you." He took some paper and a pen from his pocket.

I hesitated for a moment but then, as if under a spell, gave him my aunt and uncle's address in Westchester. "Something else," Roy added. "If things ever get tough for you, you can always take shelter in the bungalow where I've been staying. I'm writing the address and a drawing of where the key is hidden. Nobody's there except in the summer."

What a strange invitation. Why would I ever want to run away and hide myself in this spooky countryside? Nevertheless, I took Roy's note and tucked it into the pocket of my robe, suddenly wondering how I had come out to meet him so improperly dressed?

"Now," Roy said, as we stood together in the dark, "I get my goodbye kiss, something nobody can ever refuse a sailor." As he pulled me toward him, half-roughly, in a firm embrace, my resistance seemed to melt. His lips were on mine, and I was responding eagerly. My very first kiss! I gave myself up to the new sensation and to the surge of sexual feeling that swept through my body. Roy! At that moment, I believed myself madly in love with him.

We clung to each other until it was Roy who backed off. "Goodbye, you sweet girl. Think about me, huh?" His figure faded off into the darkness.

Partings, there were always partings. I lay in bed for a long time before the weeping started. It went on for a long time, until I felt a sharp poke that made me shriek and sit up in bed. Isabel! I was pretty sure that she knew I'd left the room for a time, so I lied and told her that my leg was hurting and I had gone to the bathhouse to wash the area around the wound with cool water. Then I flung my arm across my face and pretended to fall asleep.

* * *

A few days later, there was a miraculous turn of events. Late on a Saturday afternoon, Isabel was ordered by her parents to pack up her things. Although the family's stay at Shady Pines was to have lasted for two weeks, the Brandts were abruptly returning to their apartment in the city, which I had learned was on a thoroughfare in the Bronx known as the Grand Concourse.

I had just come in from a volleyball game with some of the hotel guests down on the so-called athletic field to find Isabel dashing around our room, cramming her clothes and other possessions into a suitcase that was already bulging to the point of not closing. She appeared to be having a tantrum of some kind. Startled, I inquired, "Isabel, what is it? You're leaving? Is it my fault? Where are you going?"

Without even looking up, she gave me a single word answer, "Home."

I sat down on my bed. I was hot and sweaty, and longed to go to the bathhouse to take a shower. "Isabel, please tell me. If I did something wrong, something that upset you . . . " All I could think of was my going out to meet Roy the night before he'd left. She had probably told her parents, and they had decided I was an immoral companion for their daughter. But wouldn't the Brandts have reported my misbehavior to Aunt Harriette? And wouldn't my aunt have questioned me as to my whereabouts the night I left the cabin?

"Isabel, if you won't talk to me, I'm sorry for whatever I did. But I have to go and take my shower now." I extended my hand, which she took limply. I couldn't say that I was sorry our acquaintanceship had been so short. As a matter of fact, I hoped that I would never see her again. I managed a few words: "I wish you good luck in your new school year."

When I returned to the annex room after my shower, Isabel and her suitcase were gone. Her bedding had been removed and only the bare mattress stared back at me. I dressed for the Saturday evening dinner in a pretty, aquamarine cap-sleeve dress that Aunt Harriette had bought for me in the "department store" in Harper's Falls, and wandered out onto the grounds. I was still certain that I was the reason for Isabel's departure.

Our table in the dining room had now shrunken to three places instead of six.

The arriving diners were surprised at our sudden reduction in numbers, and many stopped by to question my aunt and uncle. "I saw them pulling away in the car about two hours ago," a moustached, card-playing friend of Isabel's father remarked. "His tires were kicking up the dirt like a bucking bronco. Didn't say goodbye to nobody. What happened?"

"A family matter," Aunt Harriette replied sweetly. "Nobody sick or dying. Just a little private matter."

The unsatisfied questioner moved away hunching his shoulders, and went off to the other tables to report his non-news.

I turned to Aunt Harriette. "It was something I did that offended Isabel and her parents. Right?"

"You! Oh, no, no, no, dear."

With enormous relief, I learned that Isabel's brother Arnold, who was about to turn eighteen, had given up his plan to enter college in the fall and enlisted in the Air Force instead. Although Isabel's father was an all-out supporter of the war effort and had praised Roy generously for having joined the navy, he had hoped his own son would go to college and maybe even get a deferment. The news of Arnold's defection from civilian life that very afternoon, had resulted in Mr. Brandt's decision to cut short the family's stay at Shady Pines. They were a strange family, the Brandts, the parents often squabbling and criticizing each other, as well as Isabel. Perhaps I should have made allowances for Isabel's brusque and bossy ways? Anyway, I was now free to have my own room, to enjoy tennis on the hotel's dilapidated court, play volleyball on the bumpy lawn, go for short walks with Aunt Harriette, and to see the latest Hollywood movies at the small town movie theater in Harper's Falls.

There was also Isabel's friend, Ruth, the daughter of the Moskin family, the owners of the hotel. Although much of the placid and friendly twelve-year-old's time was taken up serving as governess for the young children of the guests, she and I had become friends. Unlike Isabel, Ruth was soft-spoken, and sensitive to others. She told me that Isabel was boy-crazy and had had a crush on Roy, whom she had already run into near the bungalow colony *before* my arrival. So that accounted, I suppose, for some of Isabel's hostility toward me. Ruth, too, admitted she was anxious to learn how to attract boys, and offered to teach me the dance rage of the day, the Lindy Hop. We spent many an evening practicing to canned music in the empty casino.

In spite of my encounter with the crazed dog, I also resumed hiking in the early morning before breakfast. One morning, I crossed the road in search of the bungalow colony where Roy had been staying. I had a vague memory of his having shown me his cabin on that awful morning when I'd been bitten. I had brought Roy's directions with me, and a good thing I did, as the cottages, all twelve of them, looked exactly alike. They were painted dark green with white shutters, and had numbers nailed to the front doors. Without Roy's note, I'd never have known which one held the hidden key.

Although it was still very early, many residents of the colony were up and about, some heading for the nearby lake to fish, so I left the grounds and continued my usual outing before returning to Shady Pines. I arrived at the hotel in a pleasantly dreamy state. I was rid of Isabel, and I would soon return to my aunt and uncle's house in Westchester, where I would attend the local high school, on a grade level appropriate to my age. I could look forward to mail from my friend Karl in England, and from Roy who, in my thoughts, had taken on a dangerous but thrilling allure.

On approaching the hotel grounds, however, my selfish meanderings fled, as it was immediately obvious that something serious was taking place. An ambulance was pulled up onto the lawn directly in front of the main building. Hotel guests and staff were milling about in a state of noise and confusion. Somewhere in their midst, I caught sight of my Uncle Herman, with his balding head and black-rimmed eyeglasses. He was waving his arms about and trying to make his way through the imploring crowd, which was apparently seeking information from him.

A pang of terror gripped me. I sensed immediately that something had happened to Aunt Harriette. I soon learned that, as in the case of Isabel and the Brandts, my aunt and uncle and I were fated to leave Shady Pines before finishing our intended stay. Although my aunt had never complained of illness, she seemed to tire easily recently. On this particular morning, she had awakened, cried out in pain to my uncle, pressed her hand to her abdomen, and fainted. An ambulance had been called to take her to the small hospital in Harper's Falls. The following day, she would be transported by long-distance ambulance to a hospital in Westchester, and my uncle and I would follow in the Cadillac. Visits to doctors would ensue, and a sleep-in nurse would be added to the housekeeping staff in the big house. My brief idyll was about to come to an end. Once again, there would be a painful parting. My guilt at having taken Helga's place seized me as never before. My life in America would be changed forever, I was sure, and I would be punished, as I deserved to be.

Eleven

At first, the cause of Aunt Harriette's stabbing abdominal pain was difficult for the doctors to diagnose. She admitted to having had gripping attacks in the past, which she had managed to conceal. "I've always hated to spoil a good time," she confessed to me as she lay in her hospital bed. Nearly a week had passed since my aunt had been hospitalized, and she was yearning to go home. "So many things to do. I want to get you some sports equipment, Helga, for when you enter high school, and ice skates for the winter. We have so many ponds that freeze over, as well as the town rink." I stroked her smooth-as-silk hand. "Don't think about me, Aunt Harriette. Just think of getting well."

The news of my aunt's impending surgery followed all too quickly. She was diagnosed with ovarian cancer, a too-often deadly form of the disease. The only hope lay in the removal of the affected organs. Her total recovery time would be six to eight weeks. This devastating news was frightening enough, before my uncle told me, confidentially, that he feared for her survival. *Arrangements*, however, had been made for me during the time of my aunt's incapacity—the Brandts had offered to take me into their apartment in the Bronx! Sally Brandt, Isabel's mother, would do anything for her longtime friend. I would go to school there, and share a room with my recent acquaintance, Isabel. My weak protests, promises that I would be no trouble if I was allowed to stay in Westchester and attend the local high school, that I wanted to be closer to Aunt Harriette in the hospital, were to no avail. Both my aunt and uncle decreed that they would be failing in their loyalty to Papa if they did not see to it that I was safe and in a good home during this trying time.

On a late-summer day, just after the start of the new school year, Mrs. Brandt and Isabel came to pick me up and take me home with them to the Bronx. The scene was Aunt Harriette's room in the hospital. Always anxious to appear bright and chipper, my courageous aunt had skillfully applied her makeup, eyes ringed as usual with black liner, eyelids shimmering with a purplish-blue hue that matched her eye color. She sat up against numerous pillows, wearing a luxurious satin bed jacket. The scent of her cologne overrode the antiseptic odor of the room. It was hard to believe that, within a day or two, she would undergo a painful and debilitating operation, as she commanded everyone, "No crying, no crying."

Isabel and I just stared at each other dumbly at

first. She finally mumbled something about having sent a postcard to Ruth and me, and apparently not having received a reply. The card, which was addressed to Ruth, had explained about Isabel's brother enlisting in the Air Force, and I'd left it to Ruth to respond. After inquiring politely about my leg, the usual nosy Isabel emerged, asking if I'd been in touch with Roy, if Ruth and I had become friends, and whether we'd been spending time together. I found Isabel's questions annoying and out of place. But I suppose she was *trying* to be more friendly than on the day when she'd swept out of our room at Shady Pines.

When the time came to say our goodbyes, Isabel and Mrs. Brandt preceded me and waited outside in the corridor.

"No crying, no crying," Aunt Harriette again insisted. "You know what that will do to my eye makeup." Choking on unspoken words, I picked up my suitcase and tiptoed out of the room to join my new hosts for the trip to the Bronx.

It was early evening when we rose up in the elevator to the fourth floor of the brick apartment building on the Grand Concourse. The journey from Westchester had involved taking a bus, and then a very hot and airless subway train. Isabel assured me that the trip took much less time by car, and wasn't nearly so exhausting.

I had never been in an American apartment. The rooms were much smaller and lower-ceilinged than the ones we'd lived in on Heinrichstrasse. The walls were painted in colors like peach and aquamarine, and the rooms were crammed with furniture. The bathroom had blue tiles and wallpaper that depicted fish swimming in and out of intricate nets. There was a lot to look at.

I was invited to sit in a very plush chair in the living room, sipping an ice-cold lemonade while Isabel and her mother bickered about something in the kitchen. As I stared at my unopened suitcase on the floor beside me, I thought of my many arrivals in many different places. Harwich, where the Kindertransport had deposited me; the Rathbone farm where Tim had been crying in the doorway; the farm hostel where I'd had my clothing burned, my hair cut, and been given a longed-for bath.

Eventually, Mrs. Brandt entered the room. "All set," she announced. "We have moved Arnold's bed from the dining alcove into Isabel's room. Once again you'll be roommates. Just like at Shady Pines, and you'll have space for your belongings. Come in, now, dear, and unpack."

The following day, Uncle Herman picked me up at the Brandts and drove me to the neighborhood junior high school, the same one that Isabel attended, to register me as a legal alien, entitled to be educated in the City of New York. I could start regular classes the very next day.

I kept telling myself how much better off I was than at the Rathbones, or at the hostel, where I'd had no schooling at all. The American junior high had a ninth grade, after which I could transfer to a proper high school. All of this education was free, and maybe I'd even be able to go on to college.

After getting me registered, Uncle Herman left me in the school clerk's office so that I could walk home with Isabel when the dismissal bell sounded. To my surprise, as I waited uneasily in these strange surroundings, the assistant principal entered the room and offered to escort me to Isabel's seventh-grade classroom. I couldn't understand why I wasn't going to be presented to the ninth-grade class, or at least the eighth, since my passport as Helga Frankfurter indicated that I was fourteen. As it turned out, the authorities at Singleton Junior High had quickly decided that my English spelling and grammar weren't good enough for a higher grade. They had put me in the same home-room as Isabel! Shades of the village school that I had attended while at the Rathbones.

But this humiliation was not the worst of it. Mr. Lockhart, the dapper little assistant principal, introduced me to the class as a new student who was a refugee from Germany. He did not mention that I was a *Jewish* refugee, and I doubt that the seventh graders even knew what a refugee was. The word *Germany* was all they needed to hear. Boos and whistles were directed at me from the back of the room, and one student raised his hand in the Nazi salute and stridently shouted out, *"Sieg Heil!"*

We walked back to the Brandt apartment through a tumult of busy streets, filled with shoppers and auto traffic. I was escorted by Isabel and her apparently best friend, Sybil, a freckle-faced redhead with corkscrew curls. The latter had brazenly attacked my attacker, an overgrown boy named Danny Brill, in the schoolyard after dismissal. (He had received only a mild reprimand from Mr. Lockhart: *Now, now . . . we'll have none of that.*) Sibby, as Isabel called her, had pummeled the chest of the towering brute, while enlightening him about my status and the awful thing he had said. She called him an "ignorant slob," and accused him of having seen too many war movies. All the while, I cowered miserably in a corner of the schoolyard, harboring bad thoughts, very contrary to what I had hoped for in America.

As we trudged home, Sybil tried to cheer me. After I sadly told her that the insult "didn't matter," she assured me that it certainly did, as America wasn't Hitler Germany. "The trouble is that most Americans still know hardly anything about what Hitler is doing to the Jews," she said. "When you meet Leona, you'll learn how little has come out in the newspapers about the Nazi death camps, and Germany's plan to wipe out the Jews and all other unwanted people."

Leona, it later turned out, was Sybil's mother. She worked in a shipyard as a welder, taking the place of the men who had been called up to fight. Not too many American women had ever done that kind of job before, and she was one of the pioneers.

I tried very hard to dismiss the turmoil of that first day at school, telling myself that Singleton Junior High was nothing but a temporary annoyance, and that Aunt Harriette would recover from her operation and I would soon be returning to live with her and my uncle in Westchester.

But when Mrs. Brandt and I went to visit Aunt Harriette in the hospital several days later—once more by subway train and bus—I was stricken by her appearance. I told myself that her shocking pallor and the sunken and sharpened features of her face were due to the fact that she lacked the energy to apply her makeup. Her eyebrows were nonexistent, giving her an almost clown-like aspect. Her lips were bare and blistered; her glistening red hair dull and matted. Although she did her best to thrust her arms out toward us with enthusiasm, it was obvious that she was extremely weak, and also drugged for pain. We had been told that the operation had gone well, but this visit filled me with anxiety. Our time was cut short when Aunt Harriette called out for more pain medicine, the nurses hurried in, and we were advised to take our leave.

* * *

That evening at the Brandts, Isabel surprised me by asking me if I knew anything about the Kindertransport.

"How did you hear about that?" I asked her.

"Hmm," she replied vaguely. "I guess it was when Sibby and I were talking to Leona. She told us you probably got out of Germany on the children's train and then sailed to England. Is that right?"

All of a sudden, Isabel appeared to care about my personal history instead of whether or not I had gotten a letter from Roy. Then I found out the real reason for her interest—she had to write a paper for her history class, and if I described my life in Hitler's Germany and my escape to England, she could get a good grade by writing about me.

Mrs. Brandt begged me to help Isabel, telling me she was a lazy student and that the only subject she cared about was French. So I told Isabel a little about saying farewell to Mutti at the railroad station, the train to Holland, and the ferry to England. She began to scribble notes and asked how to spell this and that. Mrs. Brandt, who was dabbing at her eyes with a table napkin, asked me when I had last heard from my mother. I told her it was a long time ago, and, suddenly overcome, fled to my room, where I started crying, for my lost past, my disappeared family, and now for Aunt Harriette.

* * *

I became curious to meet Sibby's mother, Leona. She sounded very aware of the world for an American, and her "man's" job in the shipyard was impressive. I could hardly imagine Mrs. Brandt or even Aunt Harriette working outside the home.

My chance to meet her came about a week later, when I received an invitation to accompany her and Sybil and Isabel to a USO club that had recently been opened in our neighborhood. I had no idea what such a club was until it was explained to me that it was an informal gathering place where soldiers who were awaiting transport to the war fronts could spend some leisure time, have coffee and sandwiches, write letters, and even get their socks mended. The "hostesses" were all volunteers and were mostly older married women, like Leona, who was thirty-five.

We all met in the lobby of the apartment building for our walk to the USO, and my first reaction to Leona was that I couldn't believe she was that old. Like Sybil, she had freckles and red hair, except that hers was rust-colored. She had dark, twinkly eyes, a friendly, slightly tough manner, and a youthful figure. She commanded me to call her Leona rather than Mrs. Simon and, as there was going to be dancing as well at the USO, she told Isabel and me to get "dressed up." So I put on Mutti's flowered chiffon dress and a pair of black patent-leather pumps with heels that Aunt Harriette had bought me.

"You're gorgeous!" Leona exclaimed the moment she saw me. "You'll be a real knockout at the club. No flirting with the soldiers, though. Even a junior hostess has to be at least eighteen. So you're *my* responsibility."

"And what about us?" Isabel piped up. "We're only twelve."

"You two, also. So behave yourselves. You can dance with each other. Anyhow, we'll be plenty busy making sandwiches and serving and cleaning up."

I was excited to go the club, as it reminded me of the thrilling weekly dances at the farm hostel, where I'd first met Karl. However, when we arrived, I discovered that the "club" was just an empty store, draped with American flags, colorful posters, and patriotic messages. Uniformed American soldiers sat around at small tables, over donuts, coffee, and soft drinks, or leaned against the food counter, smoking.

In a flash, Leona decided that the glum atmosphere needed some cheering up, so she thrust some money into the jukebox. The new Hit Parade song, *Deep in the Heart of Texas*, immediately blared forth, and everyone seemed to snap to attention. In no time, a soldier who had been smoking morosely at the counter was up on the floor, dancing with Leona. Never in my entire life had I seen such rapid rhythmic whirling and stomping. It was heart-stopping. Leona could have been in her teens, the very same age as her jazz-crazed partner. (I would learn later that she had won all sorts of dance contests in her youth.)

I was still beholding her, mesmerized, when a soldier who had been seated at one of the tables tapped me on the shoulder. I looked up at him questioningly. He was extremely tall and a little awkward-looking. I wasn't old enough to be a junior hostess. Was it really all right to ... ? Before I could say a word, he grabbed me in his arms and we were off on the floor. Soon the pulsating beat had me following his jumpy but rapid lead. Even though my heart was pounding recklessly and my head was throbbing, I was dizzily enjoying myself.

When the music stopped and a slow number came on, the tall blond soldier asked me to dance again. I said yes, and we started to talk.

"My name's Lenny," he told me. "You live around here?"

"Yes, for the time being. I really live in Westchester."

"Got no idea where that is," he said with a grin. "I'm from Montana. Missoula."

I couldn't help laughing. "I've got no idea where that is, either."

Soon, the club began to fill up with more soldiers. The volunteers—who were mainly motherly women in hairnets—bustled down to work making trays of ham-and-cheese sandwiches for Leona and we girls to pass around.

I carried a tray to the table where Lenny was now sitting with three fellow soldiers. He reached up for a sandwich and reminded me that I owed him one more dance.

"Ach, ya," I replied. "Still I am dizzy from this song about the heart of Texas. It must be crazy in that place, but I would like so much to see it."

One of Lenny's table companions looked at me suspiciously, as he caught my accent and my additional stupid and unnecessary words.

"Oh, yeah?" he said. "Where are you from anyway, girlie?"

Isabel, who was standing beside me with a tray of doughnuts, exclaimed irately that I lived right here in the Bronx with her family. The solider told Isabel she was a liar, called me a *Fraulein*, and declared, "I know a Kraut when I hear one!" adding, "What the hell's she doin' dancin' with G.I.s in a USO club?" He then rose to his feet and spat out the words, "Spying! Gathering information for the enemy! Somebody call the M.P.s!"

Lenny was also on his feet, and I watched, terrified, as he landed a crooked blow at the offending soldier's head, and then took a really hard punch in return. Instantly, a melee ensued, as soldiers from all around the room entered the fray, wrangling and hurling fists at one another. Although many bloody noses were now evident, it was doubtful that most of the participants even knew what the fighting was about. Chairs and tables had been overturned, mashed food had been smeared underfoot, and spilled coffee and soda ran in rivulets across the dance floor.

Suddenly, in the midst of the furor, a shrill whistle rent the air. The M.P.s or, as I would later learn, military police, had arrived, reminding me all too vividly of the brutal Nazi police in Germany. Even in America, I was responsible for anger and hostility, and for endangering human lives. I was reminded, as on that first day of school, that clearly I was not wanted here. Coming to America had been a terrible mistake.

With the instinct of a fleeing animal, I snatched my coat from the clothing rack and fled out into the night, with no idea—none at all—of where I was going.

Twelve

With echoing thunder and the swift passage of air, a roaring subway train entered the dimly lit station beneath the Grand Concourse and screeched to a halt. The doors slid open. A large clot of passengers emerged and others, standing behind me on the platform, began to move forward. I quickly stepped away, fearful that I might be pushed onto the train without yet being certain that it was heading north and would take me to the same stop that Mrs. Brandt and I had ridden to twice before to board the bus to Westchester.

My first instinct on fleeing the USO club before the arrival of the dreaded military police had been to head underground. Once I reached the subway station, it was a simple matter to drop my coin into the turnstile and clatter down the uneven concrete steps to the train platform. Even if I could just find my way to the hospital, to Aunt Harriette, arrangements could be made for me to be taken to her house. Uncle Herman was surely home, and Maggie, the housekeeper, was always present.

More than ever, I needed a refuge, as my stay at the

Brandts clearly wasn't working out. Singleton Junior High (Isabel called it "Simpleton") had put me in the awkward position of being in seventh-grade English, eighth-grade history, and ninth-grade mathematics. I was a stranger everywhere in the school, an odd duck who turned up here and there, had peculiar lunch hours, and couldn't seem to make any friends. And, worst of all, that first day, when I had been greeted with "*Sieg Heil,*" had become the talk of the school. Explanations that I was a Jewish refugee, a rare survivor of Hitler's murderous intentions, didn't seem to lighten the stigma. Now had come the madness that I had wreaked at the USO club. I would be sorry to lose the companionship of Leona and Sybil, just as I had been sad to say goodbye to Isabel's friend Ruth at Shady Pines. Why was it that I got along so well with Isabel's friends, and not with her?

Several trains had entered the station, coughed up their riders, taken on new ones, and rumbled away. I tried to recognize the abbreviated destinations on the cars and their route numbers or letters. But nothing seemed familiar. If only I'd jotted them down when I was traveling with Mrs. Brandt. Time was passing, my uncertainty was growing, and now, glancing down the long platform, I saw the figure of a New York City police officer. I told myself that I would board the next train wherever it was going. To be taken into custody before I could reach my family in Westchester was terrifying.

Impatiently, I stared down the track, listening intently for the distant roar that announced the oncoming linkage of clanging metal, even before the beaconed first car came into sight. At the same time, approaching quickly, was the dark-blue-uniformed officer, equipped with a gun in his holster and a swinging club, so much like those the Nazi police used to powerfully bludgeon the heads of so-called troublemakers. When I had first seen this and mentioned it to Mrs. Brandt, she had assured me that, here in the United States, these weapons were called "night sticks," and were only used on "drunkards found lying in the gutter."

"Help you, young lady?"

I turned, cowering in the presence of the puffy, red-faced officer, who seemed so much larger up close than when I had eyed him from a distance.

"I'm . . . waiting for a train," I fumbled, "except I'm not sure which is the right one."

"Yeah," he replied a bit sarcastically. "I noticed. You been walkin' up and down here a long time. Where are you aimin' to go?"

"Oh, um Westchester . . ."

"You live there?" The officer's bleary, blue eyes, sunken and red-rimmed, perused me for truthfulness, instilling a fear of oncoming doom. My deep fear of authority figures, whether the Nazi police, the ominous Mr. Rathbone, or a New York City officer of the law, overcame me. I dropped my head to avoid the officer's gaze, and gave my captor the Brandts' address on the Grand Concourse.

Isabel opened the apartment door and immediately shouted out, "She's here!" The living room resounded with exclamations of relief from Mrs. Brandt and Leona. Once released by the police officer, I ran so quickly to the room I shared with Isabel that the people in the apartment were a blur.

From behind the closed door, I heard the burly officer deliver a warning. He had at first figured me for a runaway. On being told of my German refugee status by Mrs. Brandt, he advised her to keep "close tabs" on me. "There's talk of spies getting into the country. If she finds herself in the wrong place at the wrong time, she could get into a lot of trouble." Talk of being in "trouble." I had experienced nothing but since that first day at school, where I had been teased with the undercover name of "Helga hot dog."

But far more serious to my mind was the fracas I had caused at the USO. Surely, this was only the first step in my encounters with the law in America. Bitterly, I thought again of my sins. It was not right that I should have come here instead of Helga, and the punishment I deserved was being meted out to me like small doses of poison.

* * *

A week later, there was encouraging news about Aunt Harriette. She was recuperating well, and almost ready to leave the hospital. As Mrs. Brandt was preparing for her son, Arnold, who had joined the Air Force, to come home on furlough, she assigned Isabel to accompany me on the subway and bus journey to the hospital.

Aside from going to school, I had not left the apartment since the night I'd attempted to run away. Being out in public, even with the spunky Isabel, who really knew her way around, frightened me. For some reason, I thought I would be less visible to the police if I wore one of the khaki-colored caps and jackets that I'd brought with me from the farm hostel. I had chosen a cap with a visor and put all of my hair underneath it. Isabel eyed me suspiciously, but didn't say anything about my appearance, which was surprising.

On seeing Aunt Harriette lounging in a chair in her hospital room, her hair and makeup fully restored to their former luster, my heart leaped with hope. The room bloomed with flower arrangements. Uncle Herman was there, looking much less gloomy. Aunt Harriette urged him to take Isabel and me down to the coffee shop for lunch, but Isabel stubbornly declined, saying she wasn't hungry. So my uncle and I retreated by ourselves to the cafeteria-style catery on the main floor of the building, while Isabel stayed behind in the room with Aunt Harriette.

I had always felt awkward with Uncle Herman when I was alone with him. I wondered if he, too, suffered from feelings of guilt because he had gotten out of Germany safely, and had been unable to save Papa and the rest of our family.

As we sat at a table over a lunch of soup and salad, my uncle reached into his pocket and put two letters in front of me. "A very popular young lady," he commented. "I couldn't help reading the return addresses. I see they're both from male correspondents."

I blushed and bashfully tucked the letters, one from Karl, the other from Roy, into the pocket of my jacket. They had been delivered, of course, to my Westchester address. What would I do if I never got to go back there? I could just imagine Isabel snooping around in our room and reading my letters, just as she had at Shady Pines. While Karl would have written in German, Roy had told me he couldn't spell in the language at all.

Following an awkward lunch (I couldn't bring myself to ask my uncle if he had any further information concerning Papa's fate), we returned to the hospital room. Aunt Harriette looked much more tired than when we had left. She was back in bed and her eyeliner was smudged. Had she been crying? What had she and Isabel been talking about? Sadly, I had to say my goodbyes to her, as Uncle Herman had to drive Isabel and me back to the

Bronx, where he had been invited to stay for supper on the occasion of Arnold's visit home.

When we entered the apartment, I immediately excused myself to go the bathroom—it was the safest place to read my letters from Roy and Karl. But I had to be quick. With so many people in the apartment, there was sure to be a tap on the door at any moment.

Roy's letter was on blue air-mail stationery. My heart pounding, I read:

> *Dear Sweet Helga,*
> *So you're feeling better, I hope. Boy, I can't forget how you were crying that night, especially when we said goodbye.*

My eye skipped anxiously to the next paragraph.

> *I can't tell you much about my life in the Navy. Censorship and all that, you know. But it's okay out here and I'm making some good pals. No women around, so you're perfectly safe, you sweet kid.*
> *Sure hope things work out for you in your new life in the U.S. But you seemed so scared and not sure you would be able to stay with those people who brought you over. So remember what I told you if you ever get in any kind of trouble. I showed you where the key is hid.*

Hey kid, I still don't believe that was your first
kiss. How could anybody stay away from you? So be
good, now. Close your eyes and think of me. Roy

My letter from Karl was a response to the first letter I'd written him. I had told him of my aunt's illness,
my move to the Brandts, and my unpleasant situation
at "Simpleton" Junior High School. Karl, as always, was
practical and comforting. *Do not forget how lucky you are*
to be in the free world, he wrote, *We are orphans, you and I,*
but not, thank God, in Germany!

After our hospital visit to Aunt Harriette, Isabel again
started asking me questions about my life before I came
to America. She told me that her history teacher, Mrs.
Boylan, had been delighted with her report on the
Kindertransport, and so Isabel was now anxious to learn
about my life in England. Somehow, Isabel's story didn't
sound believable. I kept thinking of Aunt Harriette's
smudged eyeliner, and how she and Isabel had been
alone in the hospital room. What had they talked about?
Was Isabel just being nosy? Or had my aunt given her
some kind of information that had raised her curiosity?

In response to Isabel's urging, I told her that the
subject was too painful to talk about just now. Perhaps I
would write it one day in German.

"In German! No. In English," she demanded. "It will

be good practice for you. And not one day. Now! Do you want to be stuck in seventh-grade English forever?"

Reluctantly, I wrote about my life at the Rathbones, in poor English and with many misspellings. I included the part about the village children throwing stones at Tim and me and shouting, *The idiot and the Jew, get off with you. No one wants you here.* But I wrote nothing about Mrs. Rathbone's cruelty in not letting me say goodbye to Tim, or about Mr. Rathbone's leering eyes, too often focused on my breasts. Isabel seemed genuinely incensed at the idiot and the Jew part. She declared that if she and Sybil and Leona had been there, they'd have "smacked them around but good."

Happily, at last, Aunt Harriette was home from the hospital! Not only that, but she and Uncle Herman planned to attend Thanksgiving dinner at the Brandts. Sybil and Leona would be there, too.

The odd (to me) American holiday was, it seemed, almost (if not more) important than Christmas. It appeared to be all about food, as for weeks in advance, the Brandts talked about the menu, which was to include a roasted turkey with stuffing, sweet potatoes, cranberry sauce, creamed onions, and cauliflower. Only the last two vegetables were at all familiar to me, from my life on the farm hostel. I had never eaten turkey or tasted a sweet potato, and I had no idea what a cranberry was.

In spite of the elaborate menu that was being planned, all I heard around me, even from Isabel and Sybil, were complaints about the shortage of butter for mashed potatoes, and of sugar for fruit pies, due to the war. Also, coffee was soon to be rationed. How innocent, I thought to myself, these Americans are. Even before I left Germany, sawdust was being added to bread flour, and "coffee" was being brewed from the roasted root of the chicory plant, and even from ground nut shells. These foods and many other products were knows as ersatz (imitation, or false).

At last the great holiday, always celebrated on a Thursday in November, arrived.

Aunt Harriette appeared, strikingly made up, garbed in a jewel-toned velvet suit, and wearing her mink coat, with hat to match. Despite these adornments, I realized how much thinner and frail she had become.

At dinner, Aunt Harriette drank several champagne toasts, along with the other adults, encouraging Isabel and Sybil and me to have "a few sips." "One day," she declared, "this terrible war will end in victory and our darlings will all grow up and have 'champagne' lives!" But despite my aunt's optimism and high spirits, she was forced, by the end of the meal, to withdraw her earlier invitation for Isabel and Sybil and me to come back to Westchester with her and my uncle for the rest of the

Thanksgiving weekend. Both Mrs. Brandt and my uncle agreed that, despite the presence of Maggie, the house-keeper, so much company would be too tiring for my aunt. So the promises of skating, horseback riding, and hikes in the autumn woods for the three of us were can-celed, and it was decided that I alone would spend the weekend at the big house in Westchester.

I packed a small bag, and we took off in my uncle's Cadillac. Sitting by myself in the back seat, I noticed that Aunt Harriette had slumped down in the passenger seat and likely fallen asleep. Her lovely fur hat of honey-toned mink slipped from her head and dropped over the back of the seat into my hands. I caressed it, with tears prick-ling my eyes, and acknowledged the unwelcome truth: Aunt Harriette's own "champagne life" was approaching its final days.

Over the weekend that followed, Aunt Harriette appeared to weaken visibly, and a private nurse was hired. On the Monday after the Thanksgiving weekend, I did not return to the Bronx for school, remaining in the house in Westchester. Miss Anderson, the private nurse, allowed me only brief visits with my aunt, claiming that "madame" must not have bad thoughts or be upset in any way.

"But I only want to comfort her," I pleaded to the snub-nosed Miss A., whose piercing blue eyes glared at me coldly through rimless eyeglasses.

When I was allowed to see my aunt, who now lay in her bed, pale, listless and drugged, she insisted on talking about my future. "You must finish school, Helga dear, no matter what the difficulties, and you must go on to college. Herman and I have talked about this, and he will see you through. And," she added, "you should seek a profession or a career, not just marriage. You mustn't be a ninny like me. I never even finished high school. I was lucky to have met your uncle. But I did nothing at all important with my . . . life." Aunt Harriette's breathing had become labored, and Nurse Anderson bore down on me like a bird of prey and shooed me out of the bedroom.

A few weeks later, on the cusp of Christmas, Aunt Harriette died at home. At the end, her sickroom was equipped with an oxygen tent and other life-saving devices, all to no avail.

The burial took place on a Sunday. It was preceded by a religious ceremony at a Jewish chapel. I had never been to an event like this before. As people began to gather prior to entering the chapel, I shrank to the sidelines. Among my aunt and uncle's neighbors, friends, and acquaintances, I knew no one. Everybody, however, seemed to know me. I was "the niece brought over from Europe." They were "sorry" for my loss. No one could have known the true depth of my sorrow. Was I destined to lose everybody—Papa, Mutti, my two sisters—and now the healing and joyful spirit of my aunt? Again, I saw this as fitting punishment for my betrayal of Helga.

As the only relatives (no one from Aunt Harriette's widely-dispersed family came to the service and burial), Uncle Herman and I sat alone in the first row of the chapel, which was reserved for mourners from the immediate family. A closed coffin of richly-carved mahogany rested on a bier beside the rabbi's pulpit. I closed my eyes to avoid the sight of the coffin, as well as that of the black-bearded rabbi, whose meaningless words had nothing in the world to do with Aunt Harriette. I doubted that he had even known her.

Once the service was over, we were instructed to get into our cars and follow the hearse to the cemetery, for the "interment." How elegant these Americans made the process of parting with the remains of the deceased. A grassy green cloth had been laid around the newly dug grave. There were more words from the rabbi, and then the coffin was slowly lowered by whispering machinery into the earth. A shovel was handed to Uncle Herman to cover the costly, burnished coffin with the first clods of earth. My turn was next, and then the shovel was passed from one mourner to the next to complete the symbolic gesture. We all left the grave site before the real covering up of the coffin began.

Following the funeral, we gathered in my aunt and uncle's house for a sumptuous banquet. A large buffet table was laden with what Mrs. Brandt explained to Isabel and me were customary Jewish funeral foods. Salty smoked fish was served to replace the tears shed for the dead, and eggs appeared on the table as symbols of the renewal of life. In addition to these, there was an array of salads, cheeses, fresh rolls, and all sorts of miniature pastries. Two hired servants and Maggie, the housekeeper, prepared alcoholic drinks and poured coffee.

The serious tenor of the mourners at the funeral had given way to a lighter atmosphere. Two of Aunt Harriette's women friends stood, cocktails in hand, admiring each other's jewelry. Uncle Herman's business acquaintances were off in a corner, chatting and drinking highballs and feasting on imported smoked salmon and black caviar. Isabel was greedily filling a plate with tiny chocolate eclairs and jam-filled tarts.

I turned my back on the self-comforting assembly, and hurried up the stairs to my room. Its cheerful flowered chintz and crisp organdy trappings, caringly designed by Aunt Harriette, were all wrong for me. I didn't belong here anymore than I did with the merry crowd downstairs.

Just for a moment, I thought of Uncle Herman. I hadn't seen him since we had returned to the house. Surely, he was downstairs somewhere among the guests?

However, I could not and would not go down there again.

Hastily, I began to pack, concentrating on warm clothes, sturdy boots, and taking along my ice skates. This time I knew exactly where I was going. I took one last look around my artificial world, the home I never deserved. Then, stealthily, dressed in a wool cap and a heavily padded jacket, I descended the back stairs at the opposite end of the long corridor of sleeping rooms, and headed directly for the railroad station.

Thirteen

A ten minute walk in the icy air of a late December day brought me to the Westchester branch line, from which I could change trains for Harper's Falls. I had learned about this from Ruth, when we were at Shady Pines. "If you're at your aunt's house this winter, you can easily get up here by train to visit us where we live in town," she had told me hospitably, explaining that the hotel itself was closed until late spring. "There's ice-skating and ski-ing just outside town. You'd have fun."

"Harper's Falls?" asked the woman at the ticket window. Even though a fire was burning in a pot-bellied stove across the room, she was bundled up against the cold. "I could sell you a ticket, but you wouldn't get there tonight. You'd have to get off to change trains at Highwater Junction. Nothing going out of there until morning."

I looked around nervously. "But I want to leave now."

"Okay by me, young lady. Only don't get mad when you sit up there in Highwater all night freezing your tootsies off. Next train out of here's in ten minutes. Want to grab it?"

"Yes," I said emphatically. I could neither go back to the house I'd just run away from, nor could I take the chance of being caught so close to the scene of my escape.

Unlike the New York City subway where I'd been shadowed by the police officer, the train for Highwater Junction came in quietly and I stepped aboard, grateful to find asylum so quickly.

To my surprise, the car was filled with soldiers, many of whom were lying across the seats in various positions of sleep. My entrance, though, seemed to cause a ripple of interest, for several of the men straightened up and patted the seats beside them invitingly. I looked around quickly to see if there were any women in the railway car. Seeing none, I took a seat beside an older man wearing glasses and sergeant's stripes. Since my experience at the USO, I was frightened of hot-headed younger soldiers. But who knew if it was any safer sitting next to a non-commissioned officer?

"Going upstate for the skiing?" my seat companion inquired by way of opening a conversation.

I nodded, fearful of even saying "yes." Suppose he picked up on my accent. Would there be a replay of the melee at the USO? I leaned back in my seat as far as I could and closed my eyes.

"Okay, miss," the voice beside me said, with a sharp thrust of sarcasm. "I guess there are some Americans who don't care to talk to the men who are ready to fight for their freedom."

His words stung, but I kept my eyes shut and willed myself into a state of numbness for an hour or so, until the conductor called out "Highwater Junction!"

The sergeant nudged me. "You getting off here by any chance, duchess?"

I quickly gathered my things, murmuring a "thank you," which must have puzzled him, and fled.

It was dark and extremely cold on the open-air platform, which was speckled with falling snow. I headed for the waiting room, anticipating a pot-bellied stove giving off welcoming warmth while I waited for the first train to Harper's Falls early the next morning. However, the coal fire had been banked and the ticket window was closed. The snack counter was covered with only a large white cloth, offering access to puny white bread sandwiches wrapped in wax paper and a variety of dried-out muffins and stale doughnuts. I pulled two chairs as close to the dwindling warmth of the stove as I could and prepared to stretch out for some real rather than feigned sleep.

While it was wonderful to be alone, without questioners and threats of being taken into custody, I wondered how safe I was, alone in the dimly lit waiting room. Although no more trains were scheduled to arrive in Highwater Junction that night, anyone from the surrounding area had access to the station. Even though the war effort was now giving employment to many Americans who had been without jobs during the Great Depression of the 1930s, there were still plenty of vagrants who slept in doorways or camped out in vacant lots. Robberies and murders committed by such people were reported in the newspapers every day.

But I could not afford to be fearful. What, after all, was I doing here? I was playing out my own death wish. I had gone as far as I could go. I believed that the end of my life in America lay before me.

The following morning, I timidly opened the door to "Roy's" cabin. Outside, no people or vehicles were anywhere in sight. The snow of the night before had stopped. The air was icy and crisp. It was a glistening, sun-drenched day. I knew at once that it would be perfect for skating on the lake that served the bungalow colony in summer.

Having arrived on the early train from Highwater Junction, I'd barely had time to examine the interior of the cottage. In the semi-dark, I had retrieved the key from its hiding place, and, once inside, thrown myself onto the nearest bed. Wrapped in all the blankets I could find, I made up for the lost sleep of the night I'd spent in the chilly waiting room. I had also brought a sandwich and a doughnut along from the Highwater Junction snack counter (for which I'd left payment).

But I soon discovered that the cabin was stocked with canned goods. Did this mean that Roy's relatives might be planning on using the place during the Christmas holiday? One thing was clear to me—I couldn't stay here long.

On departing the cottage, I noticed that my hiking boots were leaving telltale footprints in the fallen snow, a sure means of detection. All I could do was hope that the sun would quickly melt them.

I hastened on toward the wooded area that led to the lake, where I took a circuitous route that I had discovered during my visit in the summer. At last the lake came into view, crystalline and deserted. How marvelous it was going to be to skate endlessly in solitude, without the suspicious stares of our German playmates, already indoctrinated into the Nazi teachings regarding Jews.

I gave a final tug to my boot laces and shouted into the stillness, "This is for you, Helga!" There had been so many times in Germany when Helga and I had been driven off the ice, first with catcalls and later with stones. When we came home one time with bloody foreheads, Papa strictly forbade our leaving the house on Heinrichstrasse again.

As I glided toward the icy expanse before me, I could see that the lake had not completely over. Dark patches of ice, so thin that one could see the water beneath, were scattered about the spots that were covered with packed snow. I quickly mapped out a safe route, giving myself up to the joy of moving freely and lightly, as though I were disembodied. Magically, I was transported to a much earlier time, before Jews were forbidden to participate in leisure-time activities. Helga and I, as well as Mutti and Papa and Elspeth, were enjoying a family skating party. Papa was calling out, admiring our not very skillful leaps and jumps, and everyone was laughing as Elspeth fell down on her backside and kicked her little legs in the air, squealing like a piglet. How amazing! I could even hear their voices shouting, "H-e-l-g-a, H-e-l-g-a."

What did they want with my sister? She was fine, skating in loops around me, here one moment, gone the next. It was something she liked to do in her innate teasing way. There had always been a dark, unknowable side to her.

"H-e-l-g-a," again. A hoarse, urgent voice, not Mutti or Papa. And, with that, my reverie was shattered. I looked up to see Isabel struggling toward me across the ice, some of it so thin that a dropped coin would have cracked it into transparent shards. Behind her, on the shore, stood Ruth, trying to warn Isabel, as she staggered on in clumsy boots, that the lake surface was dangerous. Ruth, who lived up here year-round, knew these things. But Isabel was . . . Isabel. Even though I tried to wave her away, she continued her awkward pursuit. She wanted to talk to me. How did Isabel even know I was here? The answer came in a flash. While I'd been at Aunt

Harriette's, she had once again been snooping among my things. She had found Roy's letter and read it!

Furious, I skated away from her. She was a ruthless busybody, who couldn't keep her clutches off me or my things. Why did she even care so much? Why couldn't she just . . .

A loud crash. Isabel had fallen on the ice and was scrambling to get up, slipping and sliding, and falling down again. Ruth was screaming instructions to her. But Isabel continued to flop like a panicked baby sea lion. Foolish and reckless as she was, I knew that Isabel was now in real danger. I hastened to her side. She looked at me with wide, grateful eyes as I helped her to her feet, and carefully escorted her in the direction of the shore. For once, Isabel had taken one of her compulsions too far, and I could see that she had truly been frightened.

"Oh, Helga, thank you. But why wouldn't you listen to me before? How could you run away like that? Everybody is so worried, Helga . . ."

I glared at her, stone-faced. I had heard these admonitions so many times. Why could nobody allow me to suffer my guilt? Angry tears filled my eyes. It was time at last to spit out the truth, and take the consequences, whatever they might be.

"Listen to me, Isabel," I declared firmly, "I am *not* Helga. I am never Helga. You must not call me that again."

"If you aren't Helga, who are you?" Isabel asked, startled.

"I am Lilli," I answered "My name is Lilli. I am the elder sister of Helga . . . and I have done her a terrible injustice."

Isabel, Ruth, and I sat at the kitchen table in the comfort of the Moskin home as Ruth's mother—who cooked all the delicious meals at Shady Pines—warmed us up with hot tea and feed us her thick, buttery cookies, sprinkled with sugar and cinnamon.

Bitterly, I had thrust my Kindertransport "passport" on the table so that all present could witness my guilt. Isabel studied the photo of the real Helga, wearing a white Peter Pan collar, her dark hair cut short. "Well," she commented, "the picture's kind of muddy. But that could have been you back in 1939, before you grew your hair long. I still don't understand, though."

Painfully, I described Helga's stubbornness and her flight that day from the Bayer house, my pursuit of her, and how it came about that I broke her arm and dislocated her shoulder. The words of understanding and sympathy that I received from my three listeners only sent me into a further paroxysm of weeping into the already-sopping handkerchief that had been proffered by Mrs. Moskin. I was grateful for their kind remarks, absolving me from any wrongdoing. "But," I declared with fierce assertion, "when this war is over, I will go back to Europe, to Holland, to search for Helga and Elspeth and Mutti. I will never give up. I must find out what happened to them, and especially to Helga."

"Of course, my dear child," said Mrs. Moskin, placing her work-worn, yet surprisingly gentle hand over mine.

"Yes, you will," added Isabel and Ruth, piling their hands on top of hers. "You will."

Isabel and I sat in silence in the back seat of my uncle's Cadillac. As soon as he and Mr. Brandt had been advised that Isabel and I were safe, they had set out for Harper's Falls to collect us.

We had first driven to the bungalow colony, so that I could retrieve the belongings I had left there. "You know, miss," Mr. Brandt reprimanded, "you could have been arrested for breaking and entering. Where did you get the nerve to—"

"Staying in the cabin was all right," Isabel broke in hastily. "She knows the people who live there in the summer. They said it was okay to use."

Mr. Brandt threw up his hands. "I never heard of such a thing. Where do you kids find these so-called friends? Where do you get your ideas?" Ever since his arrival, he had been in a tizzy as to whether to scold Isabel for her bold excursion, or to praise her for having tracked me to my lair.

Uncle Herman, on the other hand, displayed his usual calm exterior. I had the sense, though, as he embraced me on his arrival and patted my back reassuringly, that he and I would soon be having a serious talk about my future. How could I possibly return to live with the Brandts? There were years of schooling ahead, and how could Isabel and I make peace with each other? I was supposed to be grateful to her for having "saved" my life when I had been so ready to throw it away. Without mentioning the unmentionable (her having read Roy's letter), Isabel tried to tell me that her nosiness about my private life was only for the purpose of understanding the war and the terrible deeds of Hitler. "I had to know all about your struggles getting out of Nazi Germany, so I could get the kids and teachers at Simpleton to feel ashamed of that awful 'Sieg Heil.' I learned so much from the things you told me. When you first moved in with us, I was such a stupid ninny . . ."

Isabel's words trailed off. I knew she was trying to apologize for her coldness at Shady Pines, and for her ongoing snooping. As to her unwanted intervention that afternoon on the lake, it had at least given me a new resolve. I would, in every way I could, fulfill my vow to one day return to Europe and find whatever remnants there were of my family.

PART III

Summer 1946

Fourteen

On a bleak morning in late June, 1946, I step out of a lodging house in Amsterdam and venture into unfamiliar streets. Having arrived in the Dutch capital only yesterday afternoon, I still don't have my land legs. In fact, in this city fortified with dikes and laced with canals, I can still feel the watery presence of my transatlantic journey from New York as a passenger on a large cargo vessel.

It was Karl who got me a place to stay here. After the war ended, he elected to remain in England. He now speaks and writes English well, and works for a refugee organization in war-battered London. His job consists of tracing the backgrounds of the Kindertransport children to see if they can be reunited with their families. *It is discouraging work*, Karl wrote shortly before I sailed for Europe. *Even though the German government has started to open up the records of the Nazi regime, chances are miniscule that parents who sent their children to Holland or to England have survived. What will we do with all these orphaned survivors? What country will take them? How will they make their futures?*

Safely tucked away in my pocket is the address of the beauty salon where Mutti was working in the months before the Nazi invasion of the Netherlands. In one of her letters, Mutti had described Margreet de Jong, the woman who owned the shop, as a member of the Dutch underground resistance. I have set out with a map of the city that marks all the streets and canals. I am shocked by the glumness and chilled by the mist that wreathes the tall, narrow houses, a mixture of shops, businesses, and warehouses, with floors that tower above them for living quarters. I assume that, like the room I am staying in at the lodging house, these quarters are cramped and claustrophobic; many of them located in attics with sharply sloping ceilings. But, of course, my view is so distorted by my American life.

After Aunt Harriette died, Uncle Herman could no longer bear to live in the big house in Westchester. Instead of my staying with the Brandts and continuing my rocky education at Singleton Junior High, everyone agreed that living with Uncle Herman in a roomy apartment on the Upper East Side of Manhattan, and attending a girls' high school in that part of the city, was a much better idea. Since I moved, Isabel and I see less of each other, but we seem to get along much better. Did it have anything to do, I wonder, with the revelation that I was fifteen-year-old Lilli instead of fourteen-year-old Helga?

As I progress through Amsterdam on this dreary morning, I become increasingly aware the war-ravaged the city around me. While Amsterdam was not bombed to rubble by the Nazi air force like the Dutch port city of Rotterdam, the streets are still littered with broken paving blocks mixed with sand and dirt. Along the canals are the crude stumps of trees that were cut down for fuel during the terrible "hunger winter" of 1944.

The few people that are out are poorly dressed, and I keep having the sense that someone is following me. When I look over my shoulder, I see no one. Yet I can't help thinking that I am furtively being peered at from this or that doorway. Perhaps it's my American clothing—a navy woolen pea coat, a beret, sturdy shoes with medium heels—the same outfit I wear on campus. Nothing showy, but I suppose it's easy to recognize that I am from "somewhere else."

With much anxiety, I finally reach the street where the beauty salon is located. Soon, I will enter the shop and meet Mrs. de Jong, to whom I had written from New York about my search for my family. Her answer was brief: *When you arrive in Amsterdam, come to the shop. Someone will help you.*

I now stand upon the very ground where Mutti and my sisters once walked. But, to my dismay, the "shop" is only a large solitary pane of smeared-over glass, making it impossible to see inside. There is no outward sign of this space ever having been a beauty salon. My heart sinks. I try the door, find it locked, and knock on it with a mixture of panic and dismay. I learned nothing from Margreet de Jong's letter, and now I've come all this way, for . . . nothing?

Suddenly, someone taps me on the on the shoulder. I turn around. He's an older man, unshaven, and shabbily dressed. I've seen several of his kind on the street. He speaks in Dutch, but the words are close enough to German for me to make out. "No good." He shakes a finger at me. "It's closed." His fingers reach out to stroke my long hair. "You want to sell?" He rubs the same two fingers together. "Good money for that. Very beautiful. I can arrange."

I shrink back in horror. Is this why he thinks I've come to the closed hairdresser's shop? To sell my hair? The Nazis brutally cut off the hair of their victims.

But the war is over now . . . or is it? Its effects seem to still be everywhere here in Holland, where there is so much poverty and need.

I turn away from the man, prepared to bang harder on the shop door. But I find it open, and am now face to face with a tall young man of perhaps fifteen or sixteen. He has a thatch of white-blond hair, and long white eyelashes. His first words are in English: "You are Lilli Frankfurter. I am Margreet de Jong's grandson, Pieter." He tells me apologetically that he was in another part of the building when I first knocked. The man who had offered to buy my hair has, of course, vanished.

Pieter invites me into the "shop," which I discover had indeed been a beauty salon at one time, as there are remnants of sinks and chairs for customers. It is also filled with mysterious cartons, as well as old brooms and mops. Were these what Mutti used when cleaning the floors littered with hair cuttings and spilled shampoo?

Pieter grins, while I stand there puzzled and helpless. "Don't be alarmed. I am here to help you until my grandmother returns. She has instructed me to see to your needs. I can show you the city."

"But . . . But when will she be back?" I stammer. My tongue has turned to cotton wool.

"In a few days," Pieter says casually.

"No!" I cry out. All of the self-confidence that propelled me to undertake this journey has vanished in a flash. "I expected to see her when I arrived. I told her the exact date. There is so much I need to know. What shall I do now?"

Pieter seems only vaguely disturbed by my outburst. "Let us go have a coffee," he suggests. He steps out into the street, and I follow. "May I take your arm?" he asks. "There are many broken walking places." Again, that grin. "It is even possible to fall into a canal. The embankments have lost their guard rails."

* * *

That night, alone in my attic room, I compose three letters: one to Uncle Herman, one to Karl, and one to Isabel that is also meant for her family (as well as Sybil, Leona, and Ruth.)

The letter to my uncle is one of reassurance, to let him know that I arrived safely and am in the care of Mrs. de Jong's family. I say nothing about her peculiar absence, which I hope is only, as Pieter said, for "a few days."

In my letter to Karl, I describe the awful ruin of the beauty salon and of Amsterdam itself, and reveal my discomfort regarding the absence of Margreet de Jong. She is, after all, a political person, involved for many years in a resistance movement that has many enemies. Even though the war has ended, Dutch Nazi elements may still be a threat to her. Or perhaps it's something quite different, and *she* does not trust *me*?

I write to Isabel on a lighter and more optimistic note. "Here I go again, Lilli, but I want to know *everything*." Isabel had implored me before I left. "Please, please write as soon as you get there." So I tell her about Pieter:

> *He's fifteen, very tall, and so blond and pale-skinned.*
>
> *He grins a lot but in a nice way. I think you'd like him. Today he showed me around the city and I was very grateful. You see, I don't care for Amsterdam*

very much. It's cold here and unfriendly, even a little frightening.

For example, I had an unpleasant surprise on my way to the beauty shop this morning. I thought I saw a telephone booth, which was sort of unusual because the city has been wrecked by the war, and it's incredibly different from New York in every possible way.

When I got closer, I noticed that the sides of the "booth" were raised above the ground and I could see a man's feet standing on the pavement. At the same time, I was attacked by the most horrible reeking odor. The "telephone booth" was a street urinal! For men. (I don't know if they also have them for women. I hope not.)

Pieter took me for coffee to a little hole-in-the-wall place that was really a bakery. The coffee was terrible. I think they use ground, roasted grain instead of real coffee, as they were doing in Germany when I left. But the freshly baked bread smelled good, and I treated us to a currant bun.

Pieter then gave me a tour of the city, and I tried to imagine what it was like before the Nazi invasion. Alas, the squares are now filled with rubble and the fountains are cracked and dry. The Rembrandt and Van Gogh museums are either closed or on short hours. The famous canal tours are not yet operating.

What things Pieter told me! In the "hunger winter"
of 1944, Amsterdammers sold their personal belong-
ings for food, they ate tulip bulbs, and the ground
was so frozen that the bodies of the dead had to be
stacked in the churches. Nor was there any wood
for coffins, as the trees had been chopped down for
firewood.

Well, I won't go into any more horrors. Tonight
my landlady gave me a supper of thick pea soup. It
was hot and filling. Tomorrow, Pieter will come and
take me to the post office to buy stamps and mail my
letters.

I am thinking of all of you at home and send my
love. Lilli

I go to bed sad and worried, after finding my way
down a dark, narrow staircase to the floor below, where
the bathroom is located.

I rise early, still feeling anxious. After a breakfast consist-
ing of a hard roll with cheese and a nameless hot bever-
age in my landlady's kitchen, I descend to the street with
my letters. I look around, but there is no sign of Pieter.
Perhaps I am too early? The few passersby in the morning gloom look at me with curiosity.

Several uncomfortable minutes that feel like hours
pass until I see Pieter sauntering toward me. My relief

is so great that I have to restrain my greeting. Pieter is grinning again. "I have good news," he tells me. "My grandmother has returned. She will meet with you in the rooms above the beauty salon. First we will mail your letters. Have you eaten?"

Starved for information only, I nod emphatically. Twenty minutes later, we are back at the messy, disguised shop, mounting two long flights of narrow stairs to an apartment on the third floor, which appears to be the home of Pieter and his grandmother.

To my surprise, the parlor room into which I am led is comfortably furnished with old-fashioned warmth. A moment later, a fleshy, ruddy-faced woman, her blonde hair streaked with gray, enters. I have to quench my impulse to grasp her hands, hands that have perhaps touched those of my loved ones.

"Excuse me for my absence yesterday," Margreet de Jong apologizes, almost gruffly. "This war," she declares, "has been a never-ending disaster, for there is now no end of matters that demand repair." She pauses to sigh heavily. "I hope you realize that your mother and sisters were among many, many refugees from Germany who came to me from 1939 on. But," she adds in a softer tone, "sit down. I remember them and I will tell you what I know."

That evening, I write an urgent letter to Karl, telling him that what I had feared most appears to be true.

After the Nazi invasion of the Netherlands on May 10, 1940, anti-Jewish measures went into effect. Dutch Jews and Jewish refugees were forced to wear the yellow six-pointed star with the Dutch word for Jew, *Jood*, sewn onto their outer garments. They also had to carry identity cards marked with a large letter J. Dutch citizens like Mrs. de Jong could no longer protect the newcomers. "I had to send Martina and the little girl to the countryside, where I thought they would be safer," Margreet de Jong told me. "As in so many cases, they were soon apprehended and sent to a Dutch transit camp. From there, trains departed daily for concentration camps in Germany and Poland. Their fate was sealed. I can't tell you more."

But, I wrote frenziedly to Karl, *Helga may have escaped.* I then tell him the amazing story that Margreet de Jong had related to me that morning, about a little-known Kindertransport that sailed from the Dutch port of Ijmuiden to Liverpool, England, on May 14, 1940, four days after the Nazi invasion:

> *Karl, this journey on a cargo passenger ship called the SS* Bodegraven, *is known in Amsterdam as "the last Kindertransport." It was organized by a brave and daring Dutch woman by the name of Gertruida Wijsmuller Meijer. She was known in the resistance and among those who were shielding*

*refugees as Tante Truus, or Aunt Trudi, for she had
long been helping children to escape from the Nazi's.*

I then share Margreet de Jong's words. "I knew
Gertruida and, when I learned of her bold plan
to put sixty or seventy refugee children from
the city orphanage on buses, bound for the only
major Dutch port still open, I contacted her
immediately to see if she could take Helga. She
was a strange child, often silent and a bit sullen.
Martina cried and begged her to go. There was
no time to lose. Suddenly she agreed. I saw her
onto one of the four or five buses, and I believe
that she boarded the ship. Others in the group
missed it, for it sailed at very short notice. And,
of course, more than two thousand refugee children in Amsterdam never had a chance to escape
after the departure of 'the last Kindertransport.'"

*Karl, my dearest friend, although Margreet de
Jong has never heard a word from Helga (and seems
quite put out about it), please give me hope that she
is still alive somewhere in England.*

*I am making arrangements to sail to England
before the week is out, and will come to you at your
address in London.*

Faithfully, Lilli

Fifteen

The taxi comes to a stop in front of a block of partially bombed-out row houses. Some are so badly damaged that you can see their naked interiors through the blasted-out windows and walls.

"This can't be right," I tell the driver. "Are you sure of the address?"

"Yes, miss," he replies politely. He repeats the street and number I've given him. "It's London, miss, after the Blitz. I could show you much worse, if you haven't seen it already."

I have seen it already. All the way from the railroad station, I've been observing fields of rubble, the skeletons of burnt-out structures, and warnings to beware of unexploded bomb sites. What made me think that Karl would be safely tucked away in some unravaged part of the city?

I pay the driver and ascend the steps of a house that is boarded up on one side, as protection against its crumbling neighbor. A petite woman with the face of an aging cherub answers the door. Amazingly, her name is

Mrs. Sweet. Karl is at work, but he has told her about my impending arrival.

She ushers me into a faded parlor, immediately offers tea, and tells me that she has a room reserved for me. "I reckon you'll want to put your feet up, dear, after such a tiring journey. Was it a very rough sea?"

"Yes," I answer. I'm still experiencing slight nausea from the crossing, so I politely refuse the bread and jam she brings along with the tea.

I've been dozing for an hour or so in my tiny room, wallpapered in a garish floral pattern that makes it seem even more confining, when there is a light knock at the door. I sit up, fully clothed, and call out, "Come in."

It is Karl. I am so happy to see him that I jump to my feet and reach out to him with my arms. He pats my back warmly during our brief embrace. I feel embarrassed. Karl and I, good friends that we were, never had any kind of physical contact. But four years have gone by since we have seen each other. In that time, I have become an outgoing American, used to casually hugging my friends. And Karl is no longer the slight figure with the noticeable limp. At twenty-one, his body has filled out and he has grown taller. In the dim light of Mrs. Sweet's rented room, I can't even make out the shiny burn scar he got when his plane was shot down over England.

Having received my letter about Helga, Karl tells me that he has already contacted the refugee office in Liverpool, requesting that they search their documents for a Helga Frankfurter who arrived from the Dutch port of Ijmuiden on the SS *Bodegraven*, a week or so after May 14, 1940. It is too early, of course, to expect a reply. Did Helga even have a passport? It is doubtful that any of the children that Tante Truus personally delivered to the crude freighter had much with them in the way of formal documentation.

Karl tells me that we should go out, so that I can become acclimated to my new surroundings. In spite of having lived in England from 1939 to 1942, I have never been to London. The shock of seeing this great city in a state of near ruin depresses me deeply.

"Ah, Lilli," says Karl, "you should also see the photos of Berlin. It has been pummeled to the ground."

As we sit in a chip shop having a meal of fried fish and chunky fried potatoes (fare unknown to us at the hostel) served on a sheet of newsprint, Karl and I talk about the idiocy of war. I declare in my new American lingo that it has been, "a crazy punch-drunk slugfest in which everyone loses."

"If not for Hitler," Karl remarks, "there would have been no need . . ."

"If not for Hitler," I repeat. And we are off again on one of our never-ending discussions about the nature of evil.

* * *

A few days go by while we wait for word from the refugee-records division at the port of Liverpool. I stroll the city and try to envision the London that I never knew. Although the weather is gloomy, as in Amsterdam, the Londoners seem to go about their business with purpose and even cheerfulness as they embark on the long road back to normalcy.

Each day I stop at Karl's office, where I've come to know several of his coworkers. I bring him baker's scones and rock cakes for his afternoon tea, or a bit of ham on a roll, whatever I can find in the shops.

One afternoon, as we are having our tea, one of his colleagues enters the office with a sheaf of photographic copies of refugee records from May 1940 that have just arrived from Liverpool. He informs us that they've not been read by anybody here. Karl and I divide the crude copies into two parts, and start to eagerly peruse the indistinct pages. It appears that hundreds of Jewish refugees without papers were aboard the SS *Bodegraven*, adults as well as Tante Truus's orphans and—with my fervent hope—Helga.

"This is odd," Karl murmurs after a while. "I have here a *Hannah Miriam Frank*. No age is given. Only: *Lodged at the Mill Road Hospital*. This is followed by a footnote: Mill Road hospital destroyed by a direct bomb-hit on 3 May, 1941."

I gasp. "No, no! That couldn't be Helga. That would

mean she escaped from Amsterdam only to die in the Liverpool Blitz. Besides, the given names are all wrong. No, I can't accept that." Tears spring to my eyes, and Karl places a comforting hand over mine.

Through a blur I finish reading my portion of the dispatches from Liverpool. Neither Karl nor I have discovered a *Frankfurter* on any of the lists. Can we really have come to a dead end?

That night, I lie in my narrow bed, mulling over the names *Hannah* and *Miriam*. Neither is unusual. Yet, I have never known a *Hannah*. There is, however, something familiar about *Miriam*. In German, Miriam is spelled Mirjam. A spark of recognition sends me into a panic. *Mirjam* was the name of Papa's mother, our paternal grandmother. She was our beloved Oma, who, along with our Opa, died in 1933, the same year that Hitler became chancellor of Germany. Helga always had a weird imagination and a stubborn will. Is it possible that she might have adopted the name *Hannah* for *Helga*, and changed the spelling of *Mirjam* to sound less German and more Jewish? I sit up in bed with a jolt. Helga may well be alive! If so, where is she now?

I am up and dressed before Mrs. Sweet and Karl have appeared for breakfast. I can't wait to test my theory out on them.

Karl appears doubtful, reminding me that we don't even know the age of this Hannah Miriam Frank and why she was lodged in a hospital on her arrival in Liverpool. I know that he is being cautious and doesn't want me to have a terrible disappointment.

"All this meandering, dearies," says Mrs. Sweet as she proudly brings a London telephone directory to the breakfast table. "I don't have a phone but I have the book. And it's current too, mind you. Look 'er up, look 'er up."

Karl glances over my shoulder as I scramble through the *F*'s. I can feel his gentle tapping on my shoulder. He is trying to calm me. Then suddenly, before our eyes, is the name: *Hannah Miriam Frank*, with a London telephone number and an address: *College of Midwives*.

A midwife! Is it possible that my sister has taken up that profession? Karl and Mrs. Sweet assure me that it's a well-regarded practice, and that the shortage of physicians during the war has led to a great demand for women who've been trained in the prenatal and aftercare of new mothers, and the home delivery of babies.

"If this person is not Helga," Karl says to me as we part ways, he to his office and I to follow up on my tormenting hunch, "promise me you'll not give up. You'll remain here and I will hunt all over England with you, if you wish." His voice is soft and comforting. Lately, I have noticed a trace of intimacy in his tone when he is talking to me, which has made me a trifle uncomfortable. I don't want the easy nature of our relationship to change, especially now when I may be so close to finding the very last remnant of my family.

Trembling with anxiety, I enter the building and approach a sober-faced older woman seated at a tall desk.

"Yes?" she says, giving me a sharp, invasive look. "Student applications are off for today. You'll have to come back next Monday. Only Mondays and Tuesdays. The course is three years. Our students live on the premises. Any questions?"

I smile as I politely advise her of her mistake, and she begins to pore through a list of student midwives currently in training. Grimly, she looks down at me. "Hannah Miriam Frank. I'm not sure you can see her right now. She is in the laboratory. You should have rung first."

"B-but," I exclaim, "I've come all the way from America . . . She is my sister, or, or she may be. You see I'm not sure. If I could just see her for one moment . . ."

My gatekeeper gives me a look of annoyance, then removes herself from her tall perch. "Come through," she says wearily, and beckons to me to follow her.

We march through a long corridor with closed doors and dark-green walls, up a flight of stairs, and through another tunnel-like hallway. My now-heavily breathing guide comes to a halt in front of a large wooden door marked *Laboratory*. She thrusts it open to reveal a well-lit room filled with work tables and sinks, snaking pipes, glass beakers, and many other sorts of laboratory fittings.

A cluster of young women in white lab coats are working, heads down, in a far corner. "Hannah Frank," my companion calls out. "There is someone here to see you."

Seven years have gone by since Helga and I were separated. The most formative period of our youth is behind us. Helga would now be eighteen; I am nineteen.

All the girls look up. One is dark-haired. She appears to be scowling as she squints in my direction.

I am shaken.

Across the gap of years, we come together. "Oh, Helga!" I exclaim as I throw my arms around her. She stiffens, then slowly relaxes.

"Lilli, where have you come from, after all this time?"

Mrs. Sweet has been kind enough to offer her parlor so that Helga and I can retrace our lives since the morning of September 1, 1939, when we said goodbye and I left with Mutti to board the Kindertransport train.

Helga insists that I go first. I tell her as concisely as I can about the landing at Harwich, my billet at the Rathbones, my days at the farm hostel, and my life in America. Also, about my current trip, beginning in Amsterdam, to search for her and Mutti and Elspeth.

What shall I tell her about Margreet de Jong's conviction that Mutti and Elspeth perished in one of the Nazi death camps? She doesn't ask. Perhaps she has already guessed the answer. Instead, she bursts out with an angry accusation: "You should know, Lilli, that that beast Koeppler arranged for our so-called escape to Amsterdam."

"I thought it was the Bayers who made it possible?"

"Both," Helga replies emphatically. "They knew it was just another death trap for us. But they wanted to separate themselves from any taint of Jewish blood. I hate them all. And I am sure that Koeppler was Mama's lover."

I've never told Helga about the night I saw Mutti in Captain Koeppler's arms. Perhaps she is right. Mutti was so desperate after Papa was arrested, she was ready to turn anywhere for help.

Helga goes on to tell me about Margreet de Jong. "She had a good heart but a stern manner. Her house was filled with refugees. She even owned the house beside it, also six stories high. On the third level there was a passageway between the buildings. She operated the beauty salon on the street level as a cover. One morning, just after the Nazi invasion, as I was helping Mama mop the floor of the shop, she came in and ordered me to immediately pack all my belongings. There were vehicles filled with Jewish orphans that were leaving Amsterdam for a ship in the harbor of Ijmuiden, bound for England.

There was no time to waste. Mama was stunned, but she begged me to go. Elspeth was playing in our back-room quarters, and she came in and started to cry. Within minutes, it seemed, Mrs. de Jong was hurrying me through the streets and I found myself in a broken-down van, surrounded by children of my age and younger. They had been told to wear their best clothes and bring along pajamas. We boarded the ship and it sailed quickly, so quickly that some of the crude transports never made it, and many children were left behind."

"That ship was the *Bodegraven*. Am I right?" I interject.

"Yes," Helga replies wearily. "We were five days at sea, and everyone was sick with the pitching and rolling. We were to cross the Channel and land at Dover. But we were fired on by Nazi war planes, and there was at least one death on board. So we changed course and sailed up the west coast of England to Liverpool. What a journey. The food was rice one day and biscuits the next. There were no washing facilities. It was cold and our bunks did not have proper blankets, only flannel bags filled with rice to keep our feet or other body parts warm. We arrived in Liverpool on May 19th, most of us without documents or any other form of identification. They took us in. A miracle!"

There was so much for me to absorb, and so many questions still to ask.

"Yes, I did get rid of the despised *Helga*," she told me when I asked about her name change. "So German!" And, yes, she had taken the name *Miriam* from our beloved Oma. Like many of the older orphans, Helga had been taken to the Mill Road Hospital, where they were boarded and given light chores rolling bandages and running errands for the floor nurses. Fortunately, Helga had been transferred to a London hospital six months before the disastrous Mill Road bombing.

At the London hospital, there had been a training program for midwives. Helga decided that being a professional midwife, responsible for the care of mothers and babies, was what she wanted to do for the rest of her life. "It's one small way for me to confront the years we have lived through," she tells me. "Now I am tired, Lilli. I will come to you tomorrow after my last class."

"Yes," I whisper. "There is so much more to talk about."

Sixteen

Karl has decided that we should celebrate my triumphal search for my sister, and has invited Helga and me to dinner as his guests at a traditional English chop house. He assures me that this restaurant will have a better atmosphere and a more varied menu, featuring hearty dishes like shepherd's pie, steak and kidney pie, and even such luxuries in these postwar days as roast beef with Yorkshire pudding, then the chip shop he took me to when I first arrived in London. When I tell Helga (she will always be Helga to me) about Karl's plan, she is agreeable, but asks if she may bring a friend along. We agree to meet at the restaurant on a Friday evening at 8:30. It's lovely to be going out for a festive meal after the lingering gloom of the war years.

I don't have any fancy clothing with me, so, as the weather has turned warm, I wear a simple frock and a small hat, tipped over one eye. Karl and I purposely arrive early and take our seats at the reserved table. He wants to order drinks from the bar, but I tell him we should wait for Helga and her young man. I am so happy that she has a "friend."

The atmosphere is cozy, with many of the tables set into curved red-leather booths with just room enough for four people to get to know one another for the first time. I am so anxious that all will go well. I cast my eyes around the restaurant, with its oak-beamed ceilings, dark-wood wall panels, and soft lighting, and my attention becomes fixed on a lovely young blonde girl with delicate features, who seems barely out of her teens. Elspeth, if she had been spared, might have grown up to look like this.

I am still preoccupied with this thought when I spot Helga, with a young woman! She has seen me and, together, they are approaching the table.

Karl and I rise, and a flurry of introductions follows:

"Helga, meet Karl"

"Karl, meet Helga."

"Everybody, meet Sophie."

Sophie is modest and soft-spoken. Helga tells us she is seventeen and also studying midwifery, but is only in her first year, one behind Helga.

As we all settle down to decide what to order, Helga remarks wryly, "This is much too elegant for the likes of us. You know, it's either baked beans or spaghetti on toast for us at school." Both young women are dressed in their student-midwife uniforms of pale blue, accented with white stripes, and they are wearing jaunty peaked caps to match.

Helga then addresses Karl. "You must have a posh job here in London," she says challengingly. "How did that come about?"

I can't help but intervene. "Karl works for the British refugee board, trying to reunite children with their families in their home countries."

Helga catches my sharp look and backs down. I had earlier informed her of Karl's background as a German airman, shot down over England, and of his enmity toward his father and all things related to the Nazi regime. But I have sensed that she does not think this former POW worthy of British hospitality.

I ask Sophie about her family and find out that she was a Pied Piper child, sent to the countryside during the London Blitz of 1941. "I was billeted with a minister and his wife in a small village," she tells me. "They were kind to me, but it was very lonely at the manse. There were no other children about and I begged to go back to my parents and my brother. My wish was about to be granted when a direct hit destroyed our home and my loved ones with it." Sophie's eyes cloud over, and Helga gives her a series of consoling pats on the shoulder, which makes me feel guilty for ever having inquired.

"You see," Helga remarks, "Heartlessness is the German way."

After that, everyone goes silent. It's a relief when the food and drinks are finally served. Helga and Sophie, obviously used to war rations, have chosen modest dishes: Shepherd's Pie and Cottage Pie, which contain minced beef and minced lamb, respectively, baked in a mashed-potato crust. Karl, on the other hand, has munificently ordered grilled Mutton Chops, and while I am trying the steak and kidney pie, which I've never sampled.

We eat quietly, making little more than small talk. I can't help noticing that Sophie frequently glances at Helga, in an almost helpless way. She says very little.

When it is time for dessert, we each go all out with regard to the hard-to-resist sweets menu: toffee pudding, treacle tart, apple crumble, and a summery cold trifle made with sponge cake, custard, fruit, and whipped cream.

When the meal is over, we all say our goodbyes and disappear into the London night. Later, I lie in my bed in the darkness of my room, thinking about Mutti and Papi and Elspeth. And Helga, and Sophie. And Karl.

The cable I sent to Uncle Herman on the day I found Helga has been answered: He is delighted that another survivor of his brother's family has been found, and he wants to know Helga's plans. Does she want to come to America, where she can continue her education, perhaps even go beyond midwifery and obtain a medical degree as an obstetrician? Wouldn't that be an achievement for a Jewish refugee child, as well as payback to the Nazis for the loss of Papa, Mutti, and Elspeth?

However, when I to talk to Helga about joining our family in New York, she tells me she doesn't want to go. "What family?" she asks. "I don't know your Isabel and her relatives and friends. As to Uncle Herman, I'm afraid he was too slow to do anyone but you much good. It's too late now. I will stay in England with Sophie. We two have been family since we met as war orphans in 1943."

I write to Isabel, who has already declared that she can't wait to meet Helga:

> *Don't count on meeting Helga anytime soon,* I inform her. *You have to understand that Helga has always been the independent sort, not wanting help from anyone. She still seems to harbor some resentment toward me, in spite of my many apologies. And I'm sure now that she doesn't like Karl. He is just too German for her.*
>
> *And then there is Sophie. Helga will go nowhere without her. In fact, she seems to have appointed herself caregiver of this waif-like creature. Perhaps Helga has always wanted such a role in her life?*
>
> *I miss you all. I will be sad, of course, to leave Karl. But I have two more years of college and I must make some kind of career for myself. Do you think I am too vainly ambitious?*
>
> *Love, Lilli*

* * *

"No, you can't think of leaving so soon," Karl says with alarm.

We are sitting on the slightly-damp grass of a park that is being replanted with trees and outfitted with new benches. I have already chosen the steamer and booked my passage. Soon after I reach New York, I will have to get ready for a July camping trip with my college sisters. In our sophomore year, six of us formed a congenial group and took up housing in one of the towers of the old-fashioned Main Building, with its austere white-walled rooms and ancient plumbing fixtures, including relics such as claw-foot bathtubs. In late August, classes will reconvene, and I'll return to the tutelage of my journalism professor, the enigmatic Dr. Barbara Bagby.

Karl knows all this. "I had hoped you might make a little more time for me, Lilli," he says sadly. "Perhaps you would come over for the Christmas holidays?"

There it is again, that vague but insistent yearning in Karl's voice that I find both stirring and disturbing. I know that our relationship has changed in these last few weeks, but I was so driven by my search for Helga that it was easy to close my eyes to Karl's subtle pleas and the growing appeal of his physical presence. Now, I suppose, whatever has been taking place between us has to be acknowledged. But before I can put this thought into words, Karl leans close to me, turns my face to his, and kisses me impetuously on the lips. "Lilli," he breathes huskily, "can't you tell? I've fallen in love with you."

I draw the hair back from my face, seeking air, space, a means of escape. But, of course, it is too late. Even though I have only *received* Karl's embrace, I know I am implicated in what is already a mutual problem.

Shy and wordless, we get to our feet and begin to walk slowly through the park.

"I know I presume too much," Karl says. "But perhaps you could continue your studies in London. I know it's dreary now, but it will recover."

The very thought of giving up my friends and family in America sends shivers through me. How spoiled and selfish I've become! Karl reads my shuddering shoulders and puts his arm around me. "All right, all right, Lilli. I am a fool. I have nothing to offer you."

We stop on the path, and I throw my arms around his neck. "No, no! You must never say that, Karl. It's just ... well, we are too young. We are so ... unformed."

"You, perhaps," Karl whispers. "I feel, Lilli, like a very old man."

We try to end the evening on a cheerier note, in a cozy, softly-lit pub. Over an ale for Karl and a lemonade for me, we sum up our situation. I promise that we will continue to correspond as before, even though I know that it will be with a bit more intensity on Karl's part, and that I must not make any careless promises simply to give him hope.

Karl lowers his voice. "I know your sister does not like me."

Impulsively, I clap my hand over his mouth. "Now, *that*," I reply firmly, "has nothing to do with us. Helga is a separate matter."

"But surely you are hurt, Lilli, that she does not want to reunite with you."

I think about this for a while. "N-o," I answer slowly. "My wish was only to find Helga alive and well. If this is the life she wants, with Sophie . . ."

"Ah, Sophie," Karl sighs. "And what are you thinking?"

"To be honest, I don't know. Maybe Helga always wanted to be the 'big sister.'"

"She wanted to be *you*?" Karl queries.

"Perhaps. Or perhaps not." I know, now better than before I found her, that parts of Helga's life will always be a mystery to me.

It is the eve of my train journey to Southampton, where I will catch the steamer for New York. Helga and I are having our second major parting, this one in her room at the College of Midwives. It's a gloomy, metallic gray, prison-like space, which she shares with two other second-year students.

"If you ever change your mind, Helga, or even just want to come for a visit ...?"

"I can see you've been converted, Lilli, to the soft life of your precious America," she interrupts. "And why not? What do they know of Nazi marching boots, of street beatings and arrests, of gas chambers and human incinerators?"

I want to tell Helga that America has been less than comfortable for me at times. But I know her mind is fixed, and further apologies or explanations will be of no use.

We have not discussed the fate of Mutti and Elspeth at length. The one thing we seem to be agreed upon is that Margreet de Jong is correct in her belief that Mutti and Elspeth were victims of one of the Nazi death camps. Before we separate, I tell Helga that I've written to Mrs. de Jong to thank her for saving Helga, and have told her about our reunion. "I think you should write to her, too," I add. "She was hurt that she'd never heard from you. If she knew you were alive, she'd be so gratified."

Helga sighs. I'm sure she knows she's been at fault. But all she says is, "If you'd ever seen the way she rushed me through the streets, holding me by the collar like some unwanted mongrel, and then hurled me up the steps of that rickety van ..."

I stand up, prepared to leave. "Oh Helga," I say in a choking voice, "you are too ... ungracious." I press two addresses into her hands; Margreet de Jong's in Amsterdam and Uncle Herman's in New York. "Write!" I order her.

She is still sitting on the bed. I can't read her expression. Her chin is cupped between her hands. Apparently, she's not going to walk me out of the building. I pause in the doorway. Perhaps there will be one more word from Helga. She lifts her head and remarks tonelessly, "You haven't said goodbye to Sophie."

Karl and I stand close together, gazing up at the ship on which I'm about to sail. It's a former British luxury liner, still disguised in its drab wartime paint, known as the "Grey Ghost" for its ability to carry troops and passengers across the Atlantic.

"Now," Karl warns, "don't go falling in love with one of those American soldiers on his way home. I hear they're a pretty wild lot." He draws me to him in an almost rough embrace. His grip reminds me of Roy's, the sailor I met at Shady Pines during my first summer in America, who I still feel somewhat attracted to, in spite of our sporadic and generally inane correspondence. These embraces confuse and weaken me. Why do I seem to melt every time I find myself in the clutches of an attractive young man? Where is my head?

The last of the "All Aboards" are being called. Karl and I kiss with intensity. I don't even know what I'm doing. Huge tears run down my cheeks. Perhaps it's the drama of departure, the human hubbub, the ship's horn sounding. Overcome with emotion, I pull away and run up the gangplank.

Later, from one of the lower decks, I look down at the waving crowd. Karl is still there, hat in hand, signaling to me. If the ship never got under way, he would stand there forever. Perhaps I am not so unformed as I think. At this moment, I feel Karl has been right for me since that moment when he waved at me from the piano in the village hall.

But how can one ever know for sure about such things?

Seventeen

At Isabel's insistence, the Brandt family is holding a welcome home party in my honor. Unlike the victorious troops who returned from the war, however, I was only abroad for a few weeks. But civilian travel is so rare these days that my exploits in Amsterdam and London appear to have been momentous—particularly to Isabel.

Uncle Herman and I drive to the Bronx on a steamy Sunday afternoon. To my surprise, the apartment is crowded with people, family, friends and strangers. Sybil and Leona are present, of course, and so is Sybil's father, the merchant seaman who had been plowing the hazardous Atlantic since the outbreak of the war. He's bearded and amiable, and I like him on sight. Arnold, Isabel's brother who was recently discharged from the Air Force, has a cuddly new girlfriend attached to his right arm, and also seems to have brought along a few of his war buddies (at Isabel's command?). And, as a special treat, Ruth has made the trip down from Shady Pines.

Even though all the windows are opened and electric fans, placed at strategic intervals, are doing their feeble best, it's stifling in the apartment. So, everybody convenes at the enormous punch bowl on the dining-room table, gulping the icy pink liquid that has limp frozen strawberries floating in it. On the table beside the punch bowl are platters of kosher corned beef and salami, sliced rye bread, and pickles and coleslaw.

In spite of eye contact and a few words exchanged, nothing seems to be happening between the girls and Arnold's war buddies. One of them confides to me that he's only interested in "older women." He tells me that "when a fella's seen action in the field, he ain't lookin' for a kewpie-doll to talk to." He traps me beside a wall and says with feigned interest, "So, I hear you been over there in the war zone yourself."

This seems a good time to politely excuse myself and duck out from under his extended arm.

I head for the bedroom that Isabel and I shared, and find that she and Ruth are already there, decrying the "drips" that Arnold brought to the party. "It is so true," Isabel declares. "You can always depend on a big brother to pick out the creepiest guys to bring home. He must have found them in a garbage can. So, okay, tell me more about this Rudy . . ."

"Oops, sorry," I mumble.

"Oh, no," the two girls cry out, scrambling to make room for me on Isabel's bed. "Ruth's been seeing this fellow all winter," Isabel explains. "And it's getting . . . well serious. We need your advice, Lilli."

"Me? Oh, what do I know?"

"You know *plenty*," Isabel bellows. At sixteen, she's grown taller and more shapely, but her twelve-year-old voice and mannerisms still hover beneath her new teen façade.

She elaborates for Ruth, who of course already knows the whole story. I, Lilli, have not one but two "boyfriends." I haven't told her much, she complains, about all the time I've spent with *twenty-one-year-old* Karl in London. Surely that must have been romantic, as we searched together and eventually found my lost sister Helga. *And*, there's always the possibility that Roy has been discharged from the Navy by now. He might in fact turn up any day.

Is Isabel psychic? She can't possibly have been snooping through my hit-or-miss correspondence with Roy, since I've been living miles from her in another borough of the city and then away at college for the last two years. Yet, it's *true*. Roy has telephoned. He just got home from overseas and wants to see me. I'm his "girl," he told me. Don't I know that? Our date is to be next Saturday night. Dinner. Dancing. Maybe a night club. Would I like that?

By this time, Sybil has joined us in the bedroom, and we get back to discussing Ruth's beau. At sixteen, Ruth has taken on a mature, almost settled air. Perhaps it's the result of all the mothering she does at Shady Pines every summer. She tells us that she and Rudy would like to become engaged and get married as soon as she finishes high school. Rudy is older, and works in his father's insurance and real estate business in Harper's Falls. He's a really good catch, she tells us.

Sybil, who's been sitting cross-legged on the other bed, emits a screech. "Married in your teens! To one of the only fellows you've ever gone out with. This is 1946. What are you thinking, Ruth?"

Isabel rushes to Ruth's defense. Everybody already knows that Sybil is transferring this year to the prestigious Bronx High School of Science, which was formerly a boys' school and is admitting female students for the first time. "Listen, Sibby, she's not some kind of math genius like you. What do you expect her to do, growing up in a small town like that?"

"Get out!" Sybil declares, her carroty-red cheeks and forehead growing livid. "Get out, look around, notice how the world is changing. Especially now, after the war."

While I am all for what Sybil is saying, I'm not so sure about the world changing for women . . . yet. Sybil will be part of a tiny female minority in the male-dominated field of science. And her own mother, Leona, has already lost her job as a welder to a returning serviceman. Real change for women may not come so soon.

When I express these thoughts, Isabel and Ruth look somewhat gratified.

They point out that there are good jobs around for women who want to be teachers or nurses.

"Yes, but those jobs have always been the professional limit for women," Sybil remarks more calmly. "The point is women just *can't* meekly return to the kitchen stove in this brand new era. And they certainly shouldn't get married in their teens. Would you, Lilli?"

"N-no," I stammer, my vision clouded by the image of Karl waving to me from the dock as the "Grey Ghost" blasted its farewells.

Dinner? Dancing? Maybe a night club? Baffled as to what to wear on my date, I eventually decide on the classic "little black dress." All the fashion magazines say that, with this standby, you can never go wrong. I arrange my hair in a French knot, fastened with some of the mother-of-pearl combs that Mutti sent me in her parcel from Amsterdam, I also wear her single-strand pearl necklace.

Uncle Herman accompanies me to the lobby of our apartment building so that he can greet Roy, who neither of us has seen in the four years since that lunch at Shady Pines. The day is still vivid in my memory: the teeth of the maddened barking dog, Roy's soothing words as he lifted me in his arms, the trip in the borrowed auto to the doctor's in Harper's Falls. I can still see Aunt Harriette fainting as I came limping toward her. (As always, I experience a throb of aching sadness at the loss of her bright spirit.)

Once again Roy has borrowed a car, an old pre-war model. I hadn't thought we'd go driving around Manhattan on a busy Saturday night. A bus or the subway would have been more convenient.

We all exchange greetings and Roy gives me an unabashed hug and kiss. I had somehow expected him to be dressed in his Navy whites, but he's in polished civilian dress, a navy blue suit and shiny satin tie. I notice Uncle Herman studying the rear of Roy's car and memorizing the license-plate number.

Like Karl, Roy seems to have grown taller and broader-shouldered in the intervening years. He slings himself into the driver's seat, lights a cigarette, and we're off, heading not downtown as I expected, but north out of the city. I feel tremulous and uneasy, and not at all as familiar as I thought I would be with Roy. He's lost that "baby-blues" look that I found so endearing during our short acquaintance.

Roy opens the window and flicks out his partially-smoked cigarette. "Has anyone told you lately? You are one beautiful lady. Smart-looking, expensive-looking, too. A lot different from that kid crying in her pajamas in the middle of the night, getting kissed for the first time. Hey, that was your first time, wasn't it?"

"Yes," I find myself replying shyly, not at all the way I want to sound. "But that was a long time ago."

"Oh yeah, I understand. You probably had lots of fellas since then that you never wrote me about." Roy leans over and presses my thigh with thick, purposeful fingers. "Huh? Huh? Come on Lilli, you can tell your old friend, Roy."

I don't like the direction that his interrogation is taking. I realize that I don't know Roy at all, that I never knew him, and that it was stupid to agree to go out with him. I try to change the subject. "So, how does it feel to be home after so long in the Navy? You'll have to tell me about your experiences. And, by the way, where are we going?" We are already out of the city limits and on one of the countrified winding parkways that lead upstate toward places like Harper's Falls and beyond.

Roy smiles dreamily and licks his lips. "I wish, kid, that I could tell you we're going to the cabin. Wouldn't that be the perfect setup? But, you know, it's summer, and a whole gang of my cousins are up there now."

I panic silently at the very suggestion. What is Roy thinking? He's no doubt become a man of the world since his adventures abroad, and perhaps, knowing I've gone abroad on my own, he thinks that I have had affairs, too.

"So," he goes on, "I thought of this neat little road-house, not too far up, that a crowd of us used to drop in on for a steak and a beer on a Saturday night. Music and dancing, too. You know, it's where Sinatra got his start."

Sinatra! It's a relief to get off the subject of the cabin in any case. "Oh yes," I remark. "Isabel and I and a friend of hers went to the Paramount Theater at Times Square to hear him sing. It was in January 1943. Girls threw their underwear to him on the stage. Bras and even panties. I couldn't understand it."

Roy turns and stares at me with a strange expression. "That's because you were this sweet, innocent kid from Europe. I'll bet it ain't that way now."

He pulls into the parking lot of a sprawling wooden building, its name strewn across the façade in bright-red neon lights, which also advertise "Dining and Dancing Nightly" and a "Full Bar." As Roy steps around the car to help me out, I find myself reliving a scene from my life in England: Mr. Rathbone has decided to stop at a roadside pub to quench his thirst. He ushers me into the unfamiliar establishment, where I eat a cheese and pickle sandwich, while he becomes blowsy and bleary-eyed. Later, he wants to rest in a "lay-by."

The roadhouse lobby is decorated in mock-rustic style with the stuffed heads of nimble, horned forest animals. Beyond the entrance is the sound of a live band and of uninhibited merriment.

Roy demands a table for two beside the dance floor and looks around with an air of satisfaction. He turns to me and strokes my cheek with lingering fingers. "When I used to come here with the fellas, we always sat in the bar. Now I'm here with my best girl. A college girl. Real class. And she gave me her very first kiss, too." Roy leans back and licks his lips again, something I don't remember him doing in the past. But how much time did I actually spend with him? And wasn't my emotional response to him based mainly on gratitude for my rescue and for being an American fighting man soon to see action? What was I even *doing* out there in the dark that night, barefoot and dressed in *pajamas*?

We argue about what I should order to drink. It's 1946, and the drinking age is eighteen, so I can't use the excuse of not wanting to break the law. Roy says an orange blossom is "nothing but orange juice with hardly any gin." But one thing I know is that I don't want to get fuzzy-headed with him.

He orders a beer for himself, a steak dinner with all the trimmings for each of us, and the next thing I know we're up on the floor, dancing jerkily to the song, "Doin' What Comes Natur'lly." As we bumble our way around the dance floor, I realize that my little black dress is all wrong. It's much too toned down and even severe. Many of the girls are wearing sweetheart necklines, off-the-shoulder frocks, even full, swirling skirts, which have been out of fashion through the shortages of the war years.

Having perspired acutely in each other's clutches, Roy and I now sit down to our drinks and dinner. From time to time we get up to dance to slower, more sentimental songs like *They Say that Falling in Love Is Wonderful* and the somewhat similar *Prisoner of Love*. "You know I am," Roy whispers wetly into my ear as we return to our table, "a prisoner of love. Hey, babe," he crushes his napkin together in his fist, "what do you say we get out of here and find a little privacy."

The final act of my evening with Roy takes place in a parked car on a side street around the corner from my apartment building. He's already made it clear that he expects a bit more than a farewell kiss, attempting to tightly squeeze my clothed nipples between his thumb and forefinger, and groping for my thighs beneath the hem of my dress. Frustrated at my resistance, he breathes into my ear. "Whats'a matter with you, Lilli. You frigid or something?"

I flare up with the indignation that's been simmering inside me all night. In a flash, I'm out of the car, rushing toward the corner of the street and the safe haven of the lobby. I greet the doorman, race for the elevator, let myself into the apartment, and hasten to my room.

My camping gear is reassuringly strewn about just as I left it, ready to be assembled for my trip next week with my college sisters. How I look forward to the upcoming getaway . . . fresh air, cool water, healthy activities, and intimate chats, exchanging views and experiences with my "group."

My senses still pounding, I grab some paper and begin a letter to Karl. I suppose I'm feeling guilty and ashamed of myself. Could anyone be more different than Roy? Karl is loyal, considerate, responsible, respectful of women, and deeply intelligent. Yet, I've promised myself that I'll make him no promises as a lover. The last thing I want is to raise his hopes and to hurt him. I still feel that the life in England that he has suggested to me may well cut off the possibilities that I look forward to in America after college. But I can't hold back.

Dear Karl, I've been thinking about one of our conversations before I left. You asked if I might come to London during the Christmas holiday season. If only there were passenger flights available, I would not have to spend so much of our time together at sea!

Perhaps winter break, between college semesters, would be a slightly longer period of time, and I could manage a crossing then. What do you think?

I proceed to tell him about my welcome-home party at the Brandts and the bedroom chat with Isabel, Ruth, and Sybil about women's futures after the war. What does he see happening in England now that the troops are home? Will women return en masse to household duties, or will they seek jobs, even professions? I thank him for his offer to "keep an eye" on my sister. Although we've both acknowledged that Helga does not care for him, it is still reassuring to have someone in occasional contact with her.

I close with more information about next week's camping trip. And, no, I do not and will never tell Karl about my first and last date with Roy! I want to end my letter with affection, not too warm, but warmer than usual.

What shall I say? Cute, modern phrases are not for Karl and me. We have never called each other by pet names. What shall I say, how shall I let him know that I have not abandoned him, that I still see him every day, waving to me in his broad and gracious manner from the boat dock. Then, a thought occurs. I will translate an old-fashioned German phrase that I have always loved. And so I write:

I send thee greetings with my whole heart.
   Your Lilli